Contents

To Chee

for saying, "I don't get it" instead of "That's really stupid."

God Has A Very Big Hat

God has a very big hat, but He doesn't wear it much anymore because it makes Him seem too tall. Every once in a while, He will put it on for an hour or so and walk around. The angels will look up and say, "Is He getting taller, or is it just the hat?"

One day He dropped the hat and it fell all the way to earth. That was the last thing the dinosaurs ever saw.

I made a copy of this hat one time, though it was much smaller, maybe 1/1,000,000,000,000 scale. One day I was wearing my God Hat replica and an unexpected gust of wind blew it off my head. It rolled down the street like a runaway train. Sparks flew everywhere. Birds fell silently from the sky. The sun stood still. The oceans turned to blood.

I never saw it again. It still gives me nightmares. I wake up looking for my hat.

I think God was trying to tell me something, but I'm not sure what.

My Psychic Friend

I have a friend who is a psychic. His business card has his name on it, and underneath it says "MIND READER." Underneath that, it says "I knew you'd say that."

When he gives his card to people, they say, "Are you really a mind reader?"

"Yes," he answers.

"Prove it," they respond.

"I knew you'd say that," he says.

Sometimes this is not enough, however, and they require more scientific proof. So they will say, "What am I thinking?"

"That I'm not a mind reader," he will answer. Sometimes, he might just answer, "How dare you!" and walk away. Or maybe slap them. Or both. But there are some people who are not so easily convinced, so my friend will say to them, "Okay, tell me what you were just thinking and I'll tell you if you are right."

I always wished I had this power, but I guess you have to be born with it, like perfect pitch or the ability to wiggle your ears. I can roll my tongue into strange and fantastic shapes, but I can't read minds. There's no money to be made in tongue rolling, but it seems like a mind reader could do pretty good.

"You should go to Vegas," I told my friend. "You could make a killing."

"No," he said firmly, and with a touch of sadness. It seems this sort of gift can't be used like that, you know, in a greedy sort of way, which I guess I understand. But I'm still impressed. Every time I call my psychic friend on the phone, he knows it's me somehow. Right away. It's amazing. Creepy, but amazing.

One time, right out of the blue, he said, "You had a dream last night, didn't you?"

"Yes!" I shouted. "Yes, I did!"

"I thought so," he said. Amazing. Even now I get chicken skin just thinking about it. I can only say I am glad he uses this power for good, and not evil. The world is scary enough.

Dream Machine

Sometimes I go to antique shops. Not because I need any antiques. I just like to look through other people's junk. It's sort of like going through someone's drawers or their mail or their refrigerator, except you don't have to feel like some kind of creepy voyeur. Once in a while I find something to buy, like a toothbrush holder or a cookie jar shaped like a hat.

One day, at a little shop in New Mexico, I stumbled across a very strange thing. It looked like an old fashioned breadbox, but it had a light bulb on top and something that looked like a metal colander attached with an old, worn out cord.

"What's this?" I asked an old man dozing in a rocker in the corner of the shop.

"Ah," he said, "that's a rare one, that is. It's a dream machine, built in '05. That's the original colander."

"What does it do?" I asked.

"It's a dream machine, ain't it? What do you think it does? It makes dreams."

"Yeah, okay. But how does it work?"

"I don't know. I ain't no scientist. But I know how to use the darn thing. See this here door on the breadbox? Well, you put whatever you want to dream about right in there. Then you slap this here colander on your head and go to sleep."

"Sounds pretty simple. How much do you want for it?"

"Six bucks."

"All I've got is four dollars and thirty-six cents."

"I'll take it."

That night I thought I'd give it a try. I put a potato in the breadbox and got in bed. I put the colander on my head and closed my eyes. "This is the stupidest thing I ever did," I thought to myself. "That old coot is probably still laughing."

But I fell asleep and had this very weird dream about being in Ireland during the potato famine. All I remember now is a bunch of guys that looked like Archie Bunker chasing me around with forks.

The next night I thought I'd give it a more enjoyable test. The potato dream could have been a coincidence. So I put an old Playboy

3

in the drawer and went to sleep. That night I had this idiotic dream that I was in a cologne ad. All I did was sit on this Corvette, try to look serious and suck in my cheeks. It went on forever.

When I got up in the morning I went to the dream machine and opened the door of the breadbox. Sure enough, the Playboy was open to an ad for some new men's fragrance, *Piston* or *Stick Shift* or something. "Wow," I said. "This thing really works!"

That night I was smarter. I opened the Playboy to the Playmate of the Month, put it in the breadbox, put the colander on my head and got ready for a very enjoyable night. "This is gonna be good," I thought, leaping into bed.

As I had hoped, when I fell asleep, there was Miss July. She turned out to be a nice, sort of normal girl. She was dressed in jeans and a very baggy sweatshirt that said "STATE" on it. She was really interested in animals and we talked for hours and hours about dogs. She had two dogs herself, Muffin, a Pomeranian, and Boo Boo, an epileptic Boston Terrier. She was doing modeling to earn enough money to go to veterinary school so she could find a cure for Boo Boo's epilepsy. She had hundreds of photos of her dogs and remembered several thousand anecdotes about each of them which she recounted in great detail, which included vocalizing the various woofs, yaps and growls of her two "babies." She was delighted to have such an attentive listener. I couldn't wait to wake up.

That morning I took the dream machine back to the antique shop. The same old man was there, rocking away.

"Hey, this thing doesn't work right," I said. "I want my money back."

"What? It didn't make any dreams for you?"

"Yeah, sure it did. But they sucked."

"I didn't say it made good dreams, young feller. I just said it made dreams. You think I'd be a sellin' a *good* dreams machine for only six bucks? What kind of damn fool you take me for?"

"Well, I don't care. I just want my money back."

"ALL SALES FINAL," he said, pointing with his cane to a 4 foot wide sign over the counter. "Can't you read?"

So that was that. Still, I didn't do so bad in the end. I got a really nice antique breadbox to keep my bread in and a perfectly working colander for four dollars and thirty-six cents. You can't beat that. And if I want to dream, I just go to sleep and take my chances. Sometimes they're funny, sometimes they're scary and sometimes they're just stupid, like the being-all-out-of-peanut-butter dream. But they're free. And I don't have to sleep with my head in a bowl.

Elvis Among the Dolphins

I bought a painting for my house last week at a flea market. It might be the greatest painting ever painted. The artist's name is Anunciatto. I don't know if that is a first or last name or where it was painted. I'm guessing Rome because it smells like *spaghetti alle vongole.*

The painting is incredible. It's very colorful. You can see the ocean from both above the water and below it. Above the water, in the distance you can see Diamond Head and the shoreline of Waikiki. There are some girls doing a hula and a guy in a lava lava doing the fire dance next to this big tiki and surfers catching a wave. It's amazing.

But it's what's *under* the water that's really incredible. There's hundreds of colorful fish, a turtle and lots of different kinds of coral. Right in the middle three dolphins are swimming. They look real. And in between two of them is Elvis, just swimming along with them. He's got that Aloha Eagle jumpsuit on that he wore the last time he played the HIC Arena in Honolulu, and a beautiful plumeria lei. The lei is sort of floating behind him because he's swimming. But he's only swimming with one hand because he's holding his guitar in the other.

The dolphins are smiling at him, I think. It's hard to say because dolphins always look like they're smiling. Elvis looks kind of serious, but you can tell he's real happy. He's not even holding his breath because his cheeks aren't pooched out.

I think the artist was trying to say something with this painting. I think maybe the dolphins are supposed to be the Holy Trinity and the ocean is heaven. Or maybe Hawaii's heaven. I don't know for sure but I think it's the artist's way of saying that Elvis is doing just fine and everybody should stop worrying about him now. Anyway it looks great in my living room.

I am saving my money to go back and get the other painting they had. I hope they don't sell it. It was the same artist, Anunciatto. This one has Elvis wearing the white Adonis suit he wore in Chicago in '72. In the back you can see palm trees and a waterfall. Above his head he's got a gold halo and you can see these big white angel wings behind him. In one hand he's holding his guitar, of course. The other arm is around the shoulder of Dale Earnhardt, still wearing his racing suit and holding his helmet. They're both smiling. Boy those Italians can paint.

Brown

I don't want to go to Mexico.
I had a dream about it
a river of a dream
brown with mud like melted chocolate.
I nearly drowned.
Just in time I came awake
gasping, fighting for breath
grasping for earth
my fingers digging into the cold, dry mattress.

Mother.

You can still see the scars from my fingernails
like furrows in the hot, brown Mexican fields
where even the weeds struggle to grow, die, and turn to brown dust.
It reminds me every day that I don't want to go to Mexico.

But I like the food.

Call Me Stupid

Okay. Call me stupid but I just don't get how this evolution thing is supposed to work. I mean, I understand the basic theory, but I just can't see it happening. It's always the same thing: some animal "needs" a long neck, so it gets one. Another needs armor-plated skin and a twelve foot tail with a spiked ball on the end, so, bingo, it gets armor-plated skin and a twelve foot tail with a spiked ball on the end.

Now I know this is supposed to take millions of years and there's really no bingo involved, but still, how does it happen? I don't know. I guess this little thin-skinned animal with no natural defenses keeps getting eaten by all the other dinosaurs and eventually some of them survive, only getting chewed on maybe, and after a while this toughens up their skin. Meanwhile, they keep whacking at the dinosaurs that are trying to eat them with their little scrawny tails (for some unknown and futile reason) and the ones that don't get eaten get stronger and longer tails. So after several million years of inbreeding these tough-skinned little guys with increasingly weapon-like tails become armor-plated Volkswagons with dangerous spiked maces growing out of their butts.

Okay. That much I can handle. But the other night I'm watching the Discovery Channel and there's this great show about prehistoric beasts, the weird as hell guys who showed up after the dinosaurs. They start talking about this gigantic, carnivorous whale, and I think, wow, this is pretty cool: a carnivorous whale the size of a jumbo jet with ten inch teeth. Lots of them. But then they say this thing started out as a land animal. Hold it right there.

I can almost believe that something crept *out* of the sea and became a land animal, but that one climbed *in* and became a sea creature is just too much. See, I can imagine an animal swimming around and looking out of the water, taking a breath of air or two, sneaking up on shore for a quick bask and then jumping back in the ocean. If animals with this taste for fresh air and dirt kept getting together, over millions of years you just might end up with a land animal. But the reverse? No way.

Take dogs for instance. For how many millions of years would you have to throw dogs in the ocean before they grew gills and stopped drowning and turned into porpoises? Someone with a lot of time and dogs on their hands should definitely check this out. I mean that's like saying birds started to fly because they kept falling out of trees and killing themselves. And this whale started out this way, right? Just kept sticking his head under water for millions of years. And drowning. So where does the breeding stock come from? They're all drowning! Someone should rethink this theory.

The Discovery Channel can say what it likes, but I will never believe that whales and dolphins started out as land mammals, went through millions and millions of years of drowning only to end up getting harpooned by Japanese and caught in tuna nets. And I *like* irony.

Everything Can Go Into an Omelet

I've discovered that everything can go into an omelet. Leftover moo goo gai pan, spaghetti, hamburgers, tuna salad, Oysters Rockefeller, chicken potpies, apple cobbler, Beef Wellington, pork chops, flan, shish kabobs. Anything.

Sometimes I'll make an omelet out of nothing but eggs and raw emotions.

Here's my favorite:

4 large eggs (or 17 if using robins' eggs, 67 if using gecko). Beat well with a sterling silver whisk counter clockwise, while humming Pachelbel's Canon in D Major. Alternate the right and left foot thusly (see illustration).

Add

1 level tbsp. anger
¼ cup chopped envy (fresh green, not dried)
1/3 cup finely minced sadness
1 tsp. hostility. If you don't have fresh hostility, you can use frozen resentment (3 tsp).
Salt and pepper to taste.

After folding, pour ½ cup (preheated) self-pity over the top. Garnish with sun-dried sympathy and serve on your best oaken trenchers. Eat with fingers only.

I find this makes a wonderful Sunday brunch when having the guys over for the big game or when simply entertaining a few old school chums that make way more money than you ever have or ever will and are wintering in Antigua (again) and think they're better than you even though they hardly have any hair left and have big pot bellies and their children hate their guts and overcharge their credit cards and a two car garage simply isn't big enough so they have to have three because the Mercedes SUV is just for the Hamptons and they just got another bonus and, well, you've got to spend it somewhere, right, you know how that is, right? Say, this omelet is good!

George Washington Crossing the Delaware

I used to be a graphic artist. It was like living in hell. At least my idea of hell anyway.

The problem wasn't that I didn't like creating designs and such. It was dealing with the people I was creating designs for. They were all maniacs. And any time you have to rely on maniacs to stay alive, it is like living in hell, which I assume is a place that's just chock full of maniacs.

See, what would happen is someone would come to my office and say something real simple like, "I need a logo."

"Okay," I would reply. "Did you have anything particular in mind?"

"No. You're the artist."

Then I would design something simple, clean, beautiful and unique. I would show it to them.

"This isn't what I had in mind," they would say.

"I thought you didn't have anything in mind," I would answer, remembering they were a maniac.

"I don't. But if I did, it wouldn't be this."

So I would say, "Well, maybe you can show me something you like to give me an idea."

Then they would return and put a print of *George Washington Crossing the Delaware* on my desk, the one where he's standing up in the boat.

"This is a little busy for a logo," I'd say tactfully.

"Really? I like it." Maniac.

So I would sit down and try to work it out. It would occur to me that Emanuel Gottlieb Leutze, the painter of this masterpiece, was probably also a maniac. George Washington obviously was. Only a maniac would stand up in a boat.

Eventually, I would get the thing done somehow. I would show it to my client.

"I think I liked the first one better," they would say. Maniac.

"You mean the one that wouldn't have been in your mind if you had one? An idea, I mean?"

"Yes, that's it."

So they would leave happy and tell all their maniac friends that I was a really great graphic designer, if you just gave me some direction. Then their friends would all come to me with prints of Titian's *Worship of Venus*, Hieronymus Bosch' s *Garden of Earthly Delights* or Raphael's *The Triumph of Galatea* and I would design a logo for their new dog food or real estate company or recirculating fan or insurance company.

They would be very pleased. I would be on the fragile rim of insanity, teetering like a drunken tightrope walker with vertigo wishing I was a forest ranger or a marine welder or something that didn't require dealing with maniacs and interpreting and translating their visions.

So I became a carpenter and started building houses. Guess what? Maniacs *live* in houses.

My Trick Dog

I had a dog once. He didn't know any tricks. Except one. He could control time.

I taught him this trick over the course of many months. Actually, it might have been many centuries, but with his ability to control time I can't say for sure. All I know is it came in handy.

Sometimes I would have a late night, playing liar's chess and drinking mai tais with the local girls at the Pearl of Hong Kong Tattoo and Massage Parlor. Inevitably, I would forget to set my alarm clock and oversleep. I would wake up and realize with something of a painful jolt that I was late for work. Again. Then I would call out, "Soren! C'mere boy!"

Soren would pad into the bedroom with his tongue hanging out like a big, wet pink sock. I think he could tell what I was going to say. He would get this really serious look on his face, for a dog.

"Soren, control time, boy. Control time. Good boy. Good boy."

The next thing I knew it would be 5:30 am and I would be waking up before my alarm even had a chance to go off. I'd take a leisurely shower, down a cup of coffee and head for work. The boss would come in and find me already at my desk, working. "I wish I had more employees like you," he'd say. "You're never late."

"It's just discipline, sir," I'd reply.

It all started when I realized Soren was getting extremely fat. I would feed him and feed him and feed him because he kept controlling time, always going back to "time to feed Soren." I finally caught on when I realized how much I was spending on dog food. But the trick was to get him to do it on command, and not just for himself.

This was not easy, because every time I'd start to teach him he'd control time and I'd have to start over. I had only one thing going for me: I was smarter than him. And I had all the food, which makes two things. He was bigger than me, being a really huge Great Dane, but I don't think it ever occurred to him to push me around. He was a good dog.

Still we had our differences. I wanted to get him neutered. He didn't like the idea. So every time I'd take him to the vet we'd end up back at the house watching *Gilligan's Island*. He never did get neutered. I guess I can't blame him for that. I did get angry with him for always making it time for *Gilligan's Island*, though. He loved that damn show.

One day I got up late again and called for Soren, but he didn't come. I called again. Finally I got up and went to the living room. There he was, curled up on the rug. He had died during the night in his sleep. I felt really bad, but I figured he probably lived longer than any dog ever had. No telling how many times he had turned the clock back. And he had died intact, which I knew was a big thing with him.

I buried him in the back yard and put an old sundial on the spot to mark his grave. Shortly after this I got fired for being "chronically late," as my boss put it. But I still find myself thinking about my trick dog, Soren. Especially when the sundial goes backwards.

Harold Tall Chief's Flying Saucer

Harold Tall Chief has a lot of money now. He used to be poor and live in this old, beat-up Airstream way out in the woods. He froze his butt off in the winter. In the summer he sweated like a fat man on the witness stand. Now he drives a Ferrari.

I hadn't seen Harold since we were teenagers, so I was sort of surprised when he emailed me one day. "Come visit" was all it said. I was going up north for the Medieval Days Festival to work the pancake booth anyway so I figured I'd drop by the trailer.

When I got there no one was home. The place looked the same as always: like a dump. There was a note on the door with directions. I got back in my car, reading them as I drove through the heavily wooded countryside.

When I reached my destination I was surprised to find myself in the parking lot of a gigantic casino. The parking lot was full and I had to pull off onto the grass. I went in the big double doors and asked if anyone knew Harold Tall Chief. "Hey, Boss!" this big guy behind the bar shouted.

Harold was happy to see me. He looked the same as ever, except that instead of his usual jeans and t-shirt he was wearing a mint green Armani suit. He still had braids and he still looked like he could kill eight or nine guys at the same time with his bare hands.

"God, Harold," I said, not believing the whole thing, "What the hell is going on? You work here?"

"Nah. I own this place. Me and the tribe. Come on, I'll give you the tour."

It was incredible. It looked like Elvis decorated it. Everything was red velvet and wrought iron. Everywhere I looked there were white folks playing slots as if they would be immediately executed if they stopped for even a second. It sounded like we were inside a pinball machine that was falling down the stairs of the Eiffel Tower.

"Wanna see something cool? Watch this," he said, digging me in the ribs and pointing to the ceiling. I looked up and there was a flying saucer, hanging from a cable. It started spinning around and humming. It had lights revolving around it that were so bright I had to shield my eyes.

"Wow, Harold," I said, "That's pretty realistic. Spielberg couldn't beat that. It must have cost you a fortune."

"Nah. Let's go in my office."

"Does Elvis live here?" I asked, looking at the reflection on the ceiling of the round red velvet bed at the far end of his enormous office.

"Of course not. Elvis is dead, man."

"Right. So where did you get that spaceship thing?"

Harold sat down in his big chair, poured us each a Jack Daniels, and passed me a cigar. He leaned back and put his big feet up on the Louis XVI desk and blew little puffs of smoke into the air that probably would have meant something significant to his ancestors.

"It was real weird," he said after some thought. "It was a couple years back. I just opened the casino and was sittin' back home in my trailer watchin' a Baywatch marathon and I hear this hummin' noise. I go outside but there ain't nothin' there.

"I decide to head back to the office to get this check I had left on the desk and as I was drivin' down the road I hear the hummin' again. I think maybe I'm havin' an ear problem, ya know? But then, I see these lights. Man, they're so bright I almost drive off into the river! Then, whoosh, they're gone! Freaked me out.

"So I get to the office and it's real creepy. See, we shut down that one weekend to fumigate so the whole place is deserted. People were getting' wood ticks on 'em and that's not cool. We're the only ones get to suck blood here. Hey, you can laugh. That's a joke."

"Oh, yeah. I get it. Funny."

"Well anyway, I'm tryin' to remember where I put this damn check and all of a sudden, these two little guys are standin' there. You know, just like you see in the movies: grey, big head, big black eyes, skinny little toothpick bodies."

"No kiddin'?"

"Yeah. No forked tongue, bro. It was wild. Anyhow, these little dudes were all turned on by this casino bein' way out in the woods. They thought it was some government installation at first, but then they get to nosin' around and watchin' everyone gamblin'. They can't figure it out. They got no concept, you know? So I tell 'em I'll show 'em around. So we go into the main room and I crank on some lights and start showin' 'em how to play the games."

"What? They were like just hanging out talking to you?"

"Well, they don't really talk. It's kinda like you just hear 'em in your skull."

"Whoa."

"Anyway, they don't care much for the slots, but the craps table makes 'em crazy. They just keep rollin' the bones and hoppin' around and making this weird little whistling noise, you know, sort of like a heron chick does when it can't find its momma."

"Weird."

"Yeah. But by now I'm getting' kinda tired of the whole thing and I'm missin' the Baywatch marathon so I tell these little dudes that if they want to keep playin' they gotta cough up some wampum. They just stare at me. I say, "money," you know. They just look at each other. Turns out they don't have money where they come from.

"So I say, well what have you got that's valuable? Then I notice they don't have any pockets. Hell, they're not even wearing any freakin' pants! So after a long discussion we decide to play for their ride. It's lucky they don't have any pants. They would have lost them, too."

"So you're telling me you shot craps with a couple aliens and won their spaceship? You really expect me to believe that?"

"Honest Injun, man. It's the gospel truth."

"And you hung it up in the casino?"

"Sure. Hey, it looks great. People get a kick outta it. Anyway, I couldn't leave it in the parking lot."

"So what happened to these guys?"

"Well they didn't *hitchhike* home. I think some of their friends musta come and picked 'em up. But they said they're gonna come back and try to win their ride back."

"How do you know they're not going to come back and vaporize the whole place or something?"

"Nah, they wouldn't do that. They're nice little guys. They were good sports about it. Anyway, I gave them a V.I.P. pass. They get a room with a hot tub and the free buffet – all they can eat. They were thrilled."

The last I heard, Harold Tall Chief still had the flying saucer in his casino. The aliens have failed on consecutive trips to win back their craft, but apparently are quite sporting about it. Harold says they told him they were working on what they referred to as "The System." "Everyone's got one," he told me with a laugh.

I asked him how they liked the hot tub and the buffet and he said they just went nuts over it. He thinks they brought some girls with them but he couldn't be sure since they all look pretty much the same. But he did hear a lot of splashing and this weird little whistling noise coming from the King's Suite that sounded remarkably like a heron chick that can't find its momma.

I Hate Clowns

I hate clowns. I have always hated clowns for as long as I can remember. This may be one reason I never ran off and joined the circus when I was a kid. I would have had to hang around clowns all day and I hate them. Never was too crazy about parades either. Too damn many clowns.

I really can't come up with a good reason for this. I have never been abused by a clown. Never even knew one. I just hate them, the way some people have a natural hatred for poodles or seafood or those big flying cockroaches or particular races they don't belong to. In this case it's definitely not a racial thing. For one, who knows what race they are under all that horrible glop? Secondly, I'm sure I would hate white, black, yellow or brown clowns with equal hatred.

The French clowns are the worst, especially the ones with the tiny hats and giant butts. It is impossible to say just how disturbing they are to me. Luckily, they mostly stay in France, where I hear the French are just crazy about them. This may be why I have no desire to go to France. I would probably be greeted at the airport by a whole troupe of these mutant clowns and lose my mind. And even if there were no clowns, the place would still be full of French people, which is almost as bad.

Then there's clown humor. I don't get it. I don't recall ever laughing at a clown or anything it did. I guess polka dot underwear just never seemed all that hysterical to me. Or falling down. Or seltzer bottles. Or pies. And the bit where they all jump out of one little car: that isn't humor, it's my worst nightmare.

Then there's the fact that clowns don't talk. They mime. To some people, this is really clever. French people mostly. To me it is just plain annoying. I want to jump up and say, "What? What? For *God's sake* what are you trying to *say?*" But this would only make the clown mime an expression of wonder or sadness or deafness or something which would make me go completely insane.

I believe in my heart that there are clowns in hell. With tiny hats and tiny umbrellas. They chase people around and mime at them. Some of them have a tear painted on their face. They run up and look at you, cock their heads, and frown, pretending to cry. They are

21

completely evil. In fact, clowns may have been created in hell for all I know, though it was probably France, which the more I think about seems pretty close to hell anyway.

Why adults think children love clowns is one of the great mysteries of life. Look at the sheer terror in a child's face when he is confronted by his first clown and you'll see what I mean. But adults don't get it, especially the ones whose relatives came from France. They will actually send these demonic creatures into rooms full of sick children to torture them with balloon animals and mimed laughter. I always thought these kids had suffered enough, though it might encourage some of them to get well faster so they can go home.

Anyway, I think there should be a law against public clowning, sort of like we have for public nudity, which I would definitely prefer any day of the week to clowning. They should round these grotesque spawn of Satan up and send them all to France, where they could fall down and spray seltzer down each other's pants and mime bewilderment to their hearts' delight. And the delight of the French, who I'm beginning to think really deserve them.

Disaster Bunny

Once there was a little bunny that lived in a little woods all by himself. He didn't have any friends and the other animals in the woods ignored him. One day the little bunny was out hopping around doing his best to entertain himself. As he was hopping along he happened to hop on a stick in the grass. This caused a large pebble to be catapulted high up into the air, right into a nest some robins were busy building. The little bunny stopped as the grass and sticks fell down on him and looked up.

"You just destroyed three days work, you horrible little creature!" screamed the female robin.

"I'm sorry. I didn't mean to," the little bunny replied tearfully.

"Well, you did. You're a disaster. Go away!"

The little bunny was terribly upset. Over the next several days, all the creatures in the little woods began to mock him, throw sticks and stones at him, and chase him away. Everywhere he went they called him Disaster Bunny. And everything bad that happened, from the turtle catching a cold to the fox stepping on a sharp thorn, was blamed on Disaster Bunny.

Then one day some thoughtless campers came to stay in the little woods. When they left to return to the big city, they forgot to put out their campfire. Instantly the dry grass began to smoke. Before long the leaves and brush caught fire and the bright red flames leapt from tree to tree.

At that very moment, who should happen along but Disaster Bunny, who was staying nearby because it was the most remote and lonely part of the little woods. Immediately he began to hop as fast as he could to warn all the other animals of the danger.

"Run, run the woods is on fire!" he shouted as loudly as he could for such a little bunny.

The robins heard his cry first and from their treetop saw the smoke and flames. They joined Disaster Bunny in alerting all the other neighbors. Soon all the animals were grouped together outside the woods. Fortunately, the stream through the middle of the woods had stopped the fire from going any further so only half the little woods burned that day. But there was no question that Disaster Bunny had saved many lives with his unselfish and courageous act.

"You truly are a Disaster Bunny," said the robin kindly. "You saved us from disaster."

So Disaster Bunny became something of a hero and a celebrity in the little woods and to the end of his days he was proud to be called Disaster Bunny and all the other animals became his friends and he was never blamed for any bad fortune ever again.

The thoughtless campers on the other hand were arrested by the local police, thanks to an observant forest ranger who saw a late model Volvo speeding away from the blazing woods. After failing a breathalizer test, the driver, who had three outstanding warrants, was sentenced to 2 years in the state penitentiary where he was killed in a freak ironing accident in the prison laundry. The other camper was sentenced to 100 hours community service and fined. He has since gone on to become a model citizen, and has put this sad but life-altering event behind him, giving fire safety demonstrations at local kindergartens in which he dresses, completely unaware of the irony, as a bunny.

I Have No Nickname

How come everyone in the world has a nickname except me? Especially people who aren't in desperate need of one? Who don't deserve one? Who have everything a person could want and then some?

Take Eva Peron for example. They called her Evita. Why the hell did she need a nickname, and why make it longer than her own damn name? She was a maniac. Then there's Ronald Reagan, the Gipper. And John Wayne, the Duke. Sinatra had more nicknames than anyone in history: Ol' Blue Eyes, The Chairman of the Board, Frankie, The Voice and Ol' Stop Hitting Me Please Frank.

Then there's Mel Torme, The Velvet Fog. Excuse me, Mel *is* a nickname. Why does he get two? Babe Ruth, same deal. Babe is a nickname in my book but somehow he rates another: The Bambino. Buster Keaton's another two nick guy. Isn't "Buster" a nickname? Huh? Oh well, let's call him The Great Stone Face just in case anyone thinks "Buster" is too formal.

Then there's all the historical guys who, though already famous, beloved, rich and the center of attention got glorious nicknames to boot: Old Hickory, Old Blood and Guts, Old Stone Face, Old Rough and Ready, Old Tippecanoe and Old Ironsides (okay, that was a boat, but it was still her damn nickname). Sure, they tacked "Old" on the front of each of these but so what? The point is they got cool nicknames and free drinks (except the boat).

And let's not forget Lincoln, Honest Abe, The Rail Splitter. Washington, Father of His Country (sure, that one wasn't real catchy, but it definitely opened some doors for him), Franklin Pierce, also known as Handsome Frank (that couldn't hurt much) and Martin Van Buren, The Little Magician. He invented that trick where you pretend to move your thumb off your hand and back on again. For that he gets a nickname.

Then there were plenty of simple ones like Silent Cal, Ike, JFK, LBJ, Tricky Dicky and Bubba (also known as Slick Willy, The Teflon President, The Zipper and The Dutch Master).

Me, I get squat. Even growing up all my friends had cool nicknames like Corky or Smitty or Sandy or Chip or Skip or Ninny or

25

Rocko or Bo or Cooter. Everyone just called me by my given name, if they called me anything at all. Hey You does not count.

I try not to be bitter but sometimes I lie awake at night imagining how much fun it would be to have a nickname. I blame my parents mostly. They did not have the foresight to give me a name that could be nicked or the personality or destiny to deserve something like Father of the Declaration of Independence or Biff.

I suppose it could be worse. I could have an embarrassing nickname like Stinky or Bed Wetter or Skunk Head or Moon Face. But you know, if people had called me Moon Face, I might have grown up to be an astronaut. I might be the head of NASA. I'll never know and now it's too late. They don't give people my age nicknames. You have to grow up with it, like your nose. It's all my parents' fault, Ol' Lefty and Honey Girl.

Instant Potatoes

I had a girlfriend once that tried to serve me instant potatoes. I don't remember her name.

"I can't eat these," I said.

"Why not?"

"Because they're fake. I don't like fake food, especially when it's potatoes."

"It's not fake. It's made from real potatoes," she explained.

"That's not the point. I like mashed potatoes made from real, actual, dirt-covered potatoes, from Idaho preferably. With little purple bruises you have to cut off. Anyway, mashed potatoes are one of the easiest things to make in the whole world. A monkey could make mashed potatoes."

"Well maybe you should get a monkey!" she screamed, revealing a surprising and unpleasant new side of her personality.

I never saw this girl again. But I did take her advice and got a monkey. And my theory proved to be correct. A monkey *can* make mashed potatoes, although they make quite a mess doing it.

The point is, if you really care about someone you give them your best. That means actually washing the potatoes, peeling them, boiling them in water and then smashing them. If you really care you will add some butter, a splash of milk, and some salt and pepper. Obviously my monkey, Randall, cares about me because he does all these things, though not necessarily in that particular order.

I hope some time down the road to have another girlfriend, but I'm not going to rush it. I have standards. She has to be pretty and she has to make real food. And like monkeys.

In the meantime Randall and I are enjoying our real mashed potatoes. I hope that girl learned to make actual food or found someone who didn't care one way or the other. She was pretty, as I remember. I was instantly attracted to her.

27

My Jellicle Cat

I have an actual Jellicle Cat, just like the ones Eliot wrote about in *Old Possum's Book of Practical Cats*. She looks exactly like the Edward Gorey illustration. Her name is Kiko. Kiko is the Hawaiian word for "spot," but she really isn't spotted. She is jellicled, black and white and "of moderate size" as Eliot so accurately described her.

The white whiskers above her eyes give her face a constantly surprised look, as if something just startled her, even when she's asleep. It's as if she were having a very remarkable dream. She might be.

Eliot seems to have had a profound understanding of cats. Of course he's not remembered for this particular asset. But "I grow old... I grow old. I shall wear the bottoms of my trousers rolled" isn't really any better than "Jellicles wash behind their ears, Jellicles dry between their toes." I put it down to literary snobbery and a general dislike of cats among the less self-assured.

I was alerted to the important fact that I owned a true Jellicle by my sister. Lucky thing, too. We don't talk that often, living thousands of miles apart and both being anti-social, but when she calls it is always to tell me Something I Need To Know. She is an artist, so I listen to her. She also likes cats and knows about these things. Someday I'll ask her to paint my Jellicle Cat, dancing in the moonlight with a surprised look on her face. The cat's face, not my sister's.

My Jellicle Cat, Kiko, actually does hop around the house "like a jumping-jack" as the poet so insightfully noted. Sometimes she hops on her back legs like she's doing a new and very vigorous feline jig. Sometimes she spins on her back like a break dancer. At other times, when the moon is just right, she hops on her front legs, looking like a moderately sized, very surprised, black and white jackass. It's amazing, and I've told her so more than once.

The other day, I learned that someone had gone so far as to make a musical about Jellicle Cats. I can't remember what it's called. They told me that since I had one of these rare and beautiful creatures, I should go to New York and see the show. I listened politely, because they were very excited and trying to be helpful. But New York is very far away and I really don't need to see the musical. I have a real Jellicle of my own. She dances just for me. And when I stand and applaud her little impromptu ballets, she always looks very surprised. I like that in a dancer.

Mangoes

I see him almost every day
inching down the road
so slowly he may not really be moving at all
stopping
for no reason and watching something.
I don't know what he's watching.
There's nothing going on.

Most people don't notice him.
He blends in with the rocks
the mango trees
the dry grass
He's very small, like a brown garden gnome,
wrinkled, burnt and bowlegged.

His clothes never change:
greenish shirt
pants that were once khaki
black rubber boots to the knees
all worn and stained
with local mud and work too hard.

He's an old man.
He told me once he made eighty.
But I'm not sure. I think he's just guessing.

You have to listen carefully when he talks.
He speaks mostly Japanese and pidgin
through a few remaining, uncrowded teeth.
He laughs a lot when he talks.
At least I think he's laughing.

He picks coffee.
It's what he does.
He carries a burlap coffee sack
to keep things in.

It's always empty.

He told me once
he hid in a tree when Pearl Harbor was attacked.
He watched the whole battle from a mango tree.
He didn't understand it then
or now.
But the mangoes were very sweet.
Juicy. Not like these.

He likes to come to the bar and have a beer
or two.
I bought him one.
Then I found out he wasn't allowed in the bar
because he pees in his pants
when he drinks a beer
or two
and it fills up his rubber boot.

They were right, but he enjoyed the beer.

I tried to give him a ride home.
He wouldn't hear of it.
He walks
so slowly he may not really be moving at all.

I watched him disappear up the road.
It was like I was sliding irresistibly backwards
or like I was being carried slowly out to sea
and he was the island
growing smaller and smaller
until he disappeared completely
and I was alone

treading water

and wondering how much sweeter a mango could possibly be.

Kona Lowell

Mr. Potato Head or Not

His eyes look like they've been stuck on with pins, and not very accurately either. His ears don't quite fit his head and if I were putting them there I would have placed them somewhat higher. They stick out like pancakes.

His mouth is lopsided, very broad and seems to be on the verge of saying something hard to pronounce. It might be "vestibule."

His head is much too big for his body. Or it may be that his body is too small for his head. He has no neck.

His arms are mere vestigial appendages. He has a Paleozoic hue to his skin, if skin it is.

His legs are made for sitting.

His pants have charisma, or is it just honesty?

His feet are capped with shoes that are perfect, significant and serene.

His mother loves him.

My Miniature Girlfriend

I have a girlfriend who's very short. A few more inches and she would qualify for midget status. She is not happy about this. She would like to be very tall, and probably willowy and blond, too, but she isn't. She's short and brunette and Chinese. As far as I know, there aren't any blond Chinese, except maybe in Northern China.

My girlfriend does not like short people jokes. She isn't too crazy about Chinese people jokes either, so I try to avoid combining the two. But I can never resist, when someone asks me, "Where's your girlfriend?" answering, "She'll be here shortly." I am usually the only one who gets it.

Actually, I think short girls are very attractive, if the rest of them isn't ugly. That and their height must be greater than their width. In her case, she's gorgeous all over and adding several more inches would just be redundant. Of course she doesn't see it this way and would like to at least be able to get things down off the top shelf without a ladder to which I say, "Fine. But then what would you need me for?"

"Other things," she says.

"Like what?" I persist.

"I don't know. Things," she says with an enigmatic Chinese smile. Good enough for me.

My girlfriend is four feet, eleven and 3/4 inches tall, but she will usually tell people she's five feet. It's a lie, but not a malicious lie. She just can't come to terms with that missing quarter inch. Another way she compensates for her small stature is by wearing heels that would give the average woman a nosebleed. It's like a magic trick when she takes her shoes off, she gets so incredibly tiny. Amazingly, years and years of being short has taught her to do almost anything in these towering shoes: run, walk, dance, drive, shop for more shoes with 5 inch heels, etc. I made the mistake once of buying her some shoes that were not tall enough. It's the only gift she has ever returned. She was not apologetic about it, either.

Even though I'm over six feet tall, we have no problems with the height difference. Except one: ballroom dancing. We just can't do it, unless she stands on my feet, which is technically not allowed in competition. But the tango just doesn't look right when the woman's head is somewhere around the man's bellybutton anyway.

Though it is a tremendous disappointment that we can never be another Rogers and Astaire, we are dealing with it. We still dance for our own amusement, with her head nestled somewhere in my rib cage, her feet planted firmly on top of mine and her long black Chinese hair tickling my knees. It's pretty great. Afterwards, when she is stretched out dozing on half the sofa, I go into the kitchen and put everything up on the top shelf.

Possibly Summer

It's the cool gray sort of day that makes you forget everything you ever knew about summer. In the distance there's something like a curtain, or maybe a wall, but if there's anything written on it, it's too far away to read anyway. It could be summer, waiting, but it's too far away to tell. It's hard to measure temperature at this distance. The fact is it's not green, but then green looks like gray when it's very far way.

There are cats going toward it, slowly, angrily, but still smiling, swinging their thin hips in time to an inaudible Egyptian mambo that's as old as murder. They might think it's summer, but they are easier to fool than most people would guess. That's not a snake: it's a string, it's a box of coat hangers, it's an old sock.

But that wall, or curtain, or maybe it's the side of a very large, old building, is something to see. It could be summer, but at this distance it's anybody's guess. The cats will be surprised. They like to be surprised. They pretend to be surprised, even when they're not. It's a snake! No: it's a pen, it's a plastic fork, it's a grocery sack. The cool gray whatever-it-is is waiting to surprise them, to jump out of the monochrome distance like a picnic lunch and be summer. The cats will be ready to be surprised even if it's not.

I am always surprised by summer, and then some. I don't pretend. I know a snake when I see one. No: that's an old tie, black and yellow and red, still poised and coiled where it fell. Red and black, friend of Jack, luckily for me. If it had been a snake I would be dead. I would be very surprised, and not pretending.

"This is heaven," they would say to me.

"I must admit I'm surprised. I was expecting summer."

"It's always summer here."

"I'm not surprised. Where are all the cats?"

"They found something they thought was a snake. They'll be along any minute now."

"What was it?"

"A tie someone dropped on the sidewalk."

"Oh. Yeah."

Rimbaud's Shiny New Bicycle

The Africans were startled. They had never seen a bicycle. Was it alive? A demon? A god? Arthur bathed in their confusion, like a pagan queen in the unpolluted blood of virgins. He wheeled through the town whistling, ignoring the stares and the dusty, dark faced children running behind him.

"*I'm swollen with harsh love's drunken torpor*," he screamed in a wild falsetto. The Africans weren't sure what this meant, but they stopped chasing him.

Instantly, he went head over handlebars, his pant leg having become entangled in the chain. The Africans approached the now prone and pitiable figure. "*I can only find within my bones a taste for eating earth and stones*," he proclaimed, wiping the red dust from his mouth and looking into their wondering faces.

"He cries for food," a young boy, who understood a little French, told the others.

"The Green Fairy, ah, she is so sweet, but not a fit companion for cycling feet I now discover with much pain and embarrassment," Arthur sighed. "Verlaine, you bastard. To this state you have reduced me, you pompous assassin of youth! You drunken pope! You pederast of piety!"

"He was a poet, a man of words," the little boy said. "The old priest told me so. Now he sells liquor and guns."

"That would explain it," one of the elders replied. "Let us help him back on his steed."

The Africans placed the delirious Rimbaud back onto his shiny new bicycle, and with a gentle push sent him rolling down the rutted, red track. Slowly he zigzagged his way down the road and out of sight, still chanting and raving until his voice disappeared in the hovering dust. There was one cloud in the African sky, the size of a dime.

"They say he was a poet," the elder told his wife. "Now he trades liquor and guns."

"Ah," she said. "That would explain it. When a man runs out of words, liquor and guns are sure to follow."

Back at the old inn, Arthur laid his bike against the peeling, whitewashed wall. His leg was sore.

"I am out of puns," he whispered. Images flew through his absinthe-clouded brain like the pages of a magazine caught in a sandstorm. He sat down heavily on the steps. In the distance a cow lowed. He thought of Charleville. He thought of milk. And breasts.

"I shall never more dance," he mumbled, wiping away one surprised tear. "And you, shiny new bicycle, mock me not! When I am yet sober once more, I shall mount you anew and ride you in fiery contemplation. Subtle monster. Have a care! There is poetry left and to spare, enough to deal with your impudent ilk."

The next day Rimbaud was seen in the village astride his shiny new bicycle. As he rode through the crowd, head held imperiously, he rang the bright silver bell. Ching-ching-ching. Ching-ching-ching. The Africans bowed solemnly as he tipped his hat.

"They say he was a poet," a man whispered to his friend.

"Ah," the other replied. "That would explain it."

Not of This Earth Shoes

One day my girlfriend went on a vacation. I really didn't want her to go, but I didn't have that much pull with her. She went anyway. So I waited. She seemed to be gone a long time. I think it was two about weeks.

When she came back, she walked into my house just as I was about to give up waiting and said, "I'm back!" With that she set a shoebox down on the table in front of me with something of a flourish. "I brought you something," she cooed sweetly.

"Thanks," I said. "I needed something to keep my canceled checks in."

"No, the present is *in* the box."

On opening the box, I found a pair of shoes. I had never seen anything like them before. They looked sort of like a cross between running shoes, sandals and court jester shoes, without the little bells.

"What are they?" I asked.

"They're shoes," she said proudly. "They're the newest style. Everybody's wearing them."

"On what planet?"

"You don't like them?" she asked, frowning. I could sense I might have hurt her feelings.

"No, no. They're really great. Here, let me try them on."

That night we went out for pancakes and I noticed that people were staring at my shoes. Apparently this style had not caught on here yet. I tried to hide my feet under the chair, but the other diners would drop their forks so they could bend down and get a better look. Later, when we were waiting for the bus, a crowd of people gathered, including a little kid who kept pointing and laughing until his mother, who was also laughing, took him away somewhere. When I got on, the bus driver asked me what nebula I wanted to go to.

"Just ignore him," my girlfriend said. "He's just jealous."

"Yeah, that must be it."

"You look great. In fact, you look very sexy in those shoes. Let's go back to your place."

So I kept the shoes, but they have not had the same effect on other women. I still have them, somewhere, although the girl that gave them to me went on another vacation. She's been gone a long time. I think it's about two years now. I hope she hasn't found me a new hat.

Kona Lowell

Sailing to Tibet

Years ago I used to live in a big city. Now I don't. I live on a mountain, way up where it's still pretty wild and people are separated by respectable distances. There's wild pigs and pheasants and turkeys. Even peacocks. But the best thing is the fog.

Sometimes I'll sit on my porch and watch it roll right up the mountain, like a soft, slow motion tidal wave, erasing everything in its path. When it reaches my house it flies past like tattered battle flags and races on up the mountain, charging fearlessly upslope like an army of Confederate ghosts.

Before long, it's all white. All the trees are gone, the sky is gone and so is the ground. My porch becomes the gondola on a hot air balloon and I'm adrift in the clouds. I pace the deck with my hands in my pockets and wonder where I'll land. Maybe Tibet. It looks like Tibet from here. Or Katmandu. I never know for sure.

Another good thing about the fog is how it makes everything look better. This only happens when it's not a complete white-out. Then I'll look at my car, parked under the big ironwood and it looks almost good. You can hardly tell it needs paint. And the little dent on the right rear fender is all smoothed out.

This got me thinking that the fog effect might be good for people, too. I could have my picture taken in the fog. I might look younger. My wrinkles would all smooth out and I would look like one of those airbrushed models in the underwear ads. And women would love it. "Come have your picture taken in our fog. Look years younger without costly surgery," the commercial would say. I bet they'd be lined up all the way down the mountain. Then as an added treat I could take them flying on my porch to Tibet. Or Katmandu. Women love that sort of thing, especially if you play a lute and sing to them while you're flying.

So now I'm working on a fog song to use on these special occasions. I want everything to be just right. The song has to be romantic, mysterious and something that goes well with fog and ballooning. And it has to be within my range. That limits me to eleven and a half notes. I think I can do it. And the fog makes my voice sound better, too. Just like Mel Torme, who is coincidentally known

40

as The Velvet Fog, except he sings about two octaves higher and can hit more than eleven and a half notes without even thinking about it.

But that doesn't matter. The main attraction here is the fog. Everyone knows that women love fog. And once we're sailing on my porch they'll be so awestruck they won't even notice that I can't sing and my lute playing is just a series of plinks and twangs. They'll be in love. They'll smile shyly at me through the fog and say, "You look just like an underwear model." And I'll say, "Thank you. So do you."

It will be great as long as the fog lasts.

Kona Lowell

She Always Dreams of Flying

She always dreams of flying
a body surfer in the clouds
the air an ocean under her
not capsuled in a metal shell
or belted in
but going where she wants to go
bird sleek and fearless as the wind that holds her up
and whispers to her things she'll never tell a soul.

This body flies.
A run, a jump and flight begins.
The rooftops peek out from the green
of trees below
gray streets meander
snake
and twist up through the hills
before the sun has warmed them up
they bask and stretch and slip away
as day begins
and waking grounds the flying girl
and brings the dreamer back to earth
the landing soft
the pillow cool
the wings are stored and put away
forgotten as the coffee perks
and work replaces reverie
She wheels herself out to the van
and plans the day and checks her notes
and messages she didn't hear but never would neglect to play.

She's not like that.

The door unlocks
the room's the same
as when she left it hours before
She microwaves the carrot cake

and in between sweet sips of tea
she nibbles it
as sleep sneaks up
she jerks awake
and picks the cat up off the floor
And now she turns the TV off
and plumps her pillow tenderly
as sleep turns darkness into sky
behind her eyelids
fluttering

Kona Lowell

Our Neighborhood Boo

When I was a little kid I used to be very frightened of this guy that lived down the street. All us kids were. We would run from him and hide when he came outside. His name was Joe.

Joe was not normal, so we were scared of him. For one thing, he was hunchbacked. For another, he couldn't talk, just make snarling noises, exactly like the Frankenstein monster. Arrr, arrrr! He had yellow fangs that stuck out and a crew cut that had a vivid V of white hair right on top. That, and the fact that he had tiny little bloodshot eyes, made him look a lot like Dracula, if Dracula were to wear khakis and a plaid shirt. He sat on the driveway, all hunched up, and sharpened knives. All day. Everyday. He drooled.

The problem was, he lived next to my best friend, so when I went across the street to play, there was a good chance Joe would be around. I would wait until he had shuffled into the garage or something to make my move, running to my friend's porch and knocking desperately. If he wasn't home I could be trapped for hours.

I remember a particularly scary dream I had about Joe when I was maybe eight years old. It seems I woke up in my bed to find that all the walls in my room had ceased to reach the floor. I could see the bushes where the walls used to be, and running around the outside of the bushes was Joe, bending over now and then to look under my walls and snarl at me. In his hand was a knife.

The odd thing was, this scary creature lived with an otherwise normal family, with a kid just a year or two younger than me. At least they *seemed* normal. I had my doubts and there were rumors of horrors Joe had committed that they kept quiet somehow. Had there really been a baby brother that mysteriously disappeared?

One day, a few years later, my friend suddenly took me to meet Joe. I don't remember how it happened but there he was right in front of me. I was terrified. My friend pulled out his pocketknife and handed it to him. He snarled a happy sort of excited snarl and took it, then shuffled off to the garage. In a moment he returned with a whetstone and began to sharpen my friend's knife to a razor edge, every so often testing it on his thumb, and snarling with approval at

44

the progress. I noticed that his thumb was a network of scars. I gave him my knife. Arrr, arrrr!

I was small for my age, but I realized at that moment how small Joe was. He was a tiny little man, maybe all of five feet tall. He had tiny feet and delicate little hands. His khaki trousers were neatly pressed and his plaid J. C. Penny shirt was clean and ironed. He had brown wingtips on his tiny feet, polished with military dedication. He had cut himself shaving and had a little Band-Aid on his neck.

Joe had dozens of knives, which he took out and showed us with great pride and excitement. He handed me one: a small silver and black pocketknife. I took it and opened the blade. It was sharp enough to shave with. I closed it and handed it back to him, but he snarled and waived his hand like he was shooing away something unpleasant. It was a gift. I took it.

Joe still had a hump on his back, yellow fangs and Dracula hair, but I wasn't scared of him after that. I would say, "Hi, Joe," when I went to visit my friend. He would wave and snarl as he crouched on the driveway, sharpening his knife. If the football went in his yard, he'd throw it back as best he could. And we'd always show him our new knives to his great delight.

I guess this is when I started wondering what else I was scared of for no good reason. And it occurred to me, if Joe could face the world with all his limitations, why couldn't I? Sure, I was small, skinny and easy to beat up, but I wasn't hunchbacked, could talk, had at least normal intelligence and would eventually get taller. I don't think anyone has really scared me since then.

I lost the little silver and black knife Joe gave me years ago.

The Atheist Who Couldn't Swear Too Good

One day when I was driving to the grocery store to get some socks, I accidentally cut another car off. I guess my mind was somewhere else. I was thinking about my new socks and sort of mentally rearranging my sock drawer to accommodate the newcomers. I didn't notice he had gone into a ditch. I just saw him waving at me.

Anyway, this guy was awful mad. I had pulled over thinking I had won something maybe, because he looked just like Ed McMahon. I guess I was pretty excited about all the socks I would be able to afford. I mean really good socks, like David Niven might have worn, or even Bobby Darin.

But it turned out not to be Ed McMahon and like I said, this guy was really mad. I rolled down my window and said, "What's the problem?"

"The problem? I'll tell you what the nothing-damned problem is you nothing-damned idiot! You just ran me off the nothing-damned road!"

"Huh?"

"You heard me!"

"Sorry," I said, and really meant it. "I was thinking about my socks. You know how it is. But I don't quite follow your cursing."

"What?"

"You know, the 'nothing-damned' part. I don't get it."

"Oh, go to someplace that doesn't exist!"

With that he got back in his Buick, slammed the door and peeled off, creating a glorious pheasant tail of dust and gravel behind him. I sat there for a while trying to think of some place that didn't exist but gave it up. It was the least effective cussing-out I had ever had. I felt really bad for him.

But the delay caused by this short confrontation proved real lucky for me after all. When I went in the grocery store they were *just at that very minute* changing the price on the socks I had been saving up for. I got two pairs for the price of one. And these weren't just ordinary socks, but the sheer kind you can see your skin through. Exactly like David Niven might have worn, or even Bobby Darin.

Suddenly Mortal

When I was a kid I thought I was immortal. Not like a god or something, but like nothing bad could ever happen to me. Because of this, I did all sorts of dangerous things. My friends were even more convinced that they were immortal, and as a result I would get talked into doing really stupidly dangerous stuff. Usually they accomplished this by calling me a "baby" or a "woosie." Somehow I survived, thank God.

Since this all happened before computers and video games, we were outdoor kids. Our parents wouldn't let us in the house very often, except to eat and brush our teeth. In the summer, we even slept outside in the back yard. We called it "camping out." I don't know what our parents called it, but they never had to be talked into this for some reason. In fact they would suggest this "adventure" every weekend until about the first snow.

Because we spent all our time outside, we eventually got tired of baseball and football and created other pastimes. Jumping off the roof was a good one. Hopping on the back of milk trucks and riding down the highway was another. Sneaking into the pasture and riding horses with no bridle till they dumped us off was fun, too. But climbing things that were way too tall was our favorite.

After a while we had climbed all the biggest trees, so we went exploring and eventually discovered The Cliffs. These were very tall (at least to kids) limestone bluffs that were in an upscale neighborhood a good bike ride away. At the base of these cliffs was a boulder-filled creek with pretty good fishing. The creek ran for miles, under bridges, through the woods, and through different parts of town. Sometimes we'd make a raft and float down it, fishing. Like Tom Sawyer, we thought. People used to drown in it all the time.

But our main thrill was climbing the cliffs. I don't know how tall they really were, but it looked like a long way down when you were on top. The creek looked very small down below and the big boulders looked like pebbles.

It was difficult to get to the top. It was worse coming down. The limestone was slippery with fallen leaves and would break under your feet. To remedy this problem we attached a long length of very old and decaying garden hose to a chain link fence at the top. That way we could climb most of the way up the cliff, grab the hose and use it to climb up the rest of the way. We could also repel back down on this deteriorating hose and swing in big arcs across the cliff face.

The last time I climbed the cliffs, I had just reached the ground and was making my way across the creek, from boulder to boulder back to the far shore. Some friends of mine were still at the top. Suddenly one of them slipped. I don't think he screamed. I remember being unable to move. He slid some ways down on his back. Then he hit an outcropping of limestone and did a perfect swan dive. When he hit the boulders next to me, he bounced. I was amazed at that bounce, and still am.

No one moved. We all stood like childish statues, me in the creek, some on boulders, some in water up to their knees, some still at the top. To this day I don't know how they ever climbed down. Suddenly the spell was broken. Our friend sat up, covered in blood. He said, "Ow," then collapsed. Immediately we were running, looking for help. Some of us just ran and hid. Some are probably still running.

Amazingly, our friend survived, though he had compound fractures of almost every limb. I never saw him again but I heard he was eventually okay.

I never climbed the cliffs again. I could say that I don't like heights, but that wouldn't really cover it. I can still see that kid sliding down, desperately trying to stop, as his jeans wore through to the bone. I can still see the look on his face, the question, the surprise and the complete and utter terror. I can hear the slithering rock and debris as it splashed and clattered in the water and on the rocks below. I can still see the perfect swan dive into breathless, empty space and the unexpected bounce when he hit ten feet from where I stood, frozen, afraid, suddenly and forever aware of my own very real, very fragile mortality.

We never talked about this, us kids. I think it hit each of us differently. Now if we ever bring it up, reminiscing as old friends do over a beer or two, we still don't have much to say. It was a hard lesson. It remains a tough memory. But none of us doubt that we are fortunate to be here. We did some really stupid stuff. We should all be dead, but we're not. It was great being a kid.

The Cigarette Cat

You probably won't believe this story, but it's true. Really. Even if everything else I've ever said is a complete lie, this isn't.

I had a fluffy white cat named Sweety. No, that's not the part that's hard to believe. That's the part that was hard to live with. I never did get used to standing in my yard screaming "Sweety" at the top of my lungs. My neighbors thought I was weird enough already. But I didn't name her and everyone knows you can't change a cat's name. They get very angry and confused if you do. That can lead to Cat Vengeance which can be pretty disgusting, especially if they do it in your shoe.

When Sweety was a kitten, I used to wad up an empty cigarette pack and throw it for her. She loved this and would skitter after it and bring it back to me, drop it at my feet, and wait for me to throw it again. Just like a dog, except she didn't slobber on it. We did this for hours. We both had a lot of free time back then.

Now here comes the part you won't believe.

I guess this cigarette pack chasing must have had an effect on Sweety. Maybe she liked the smell of tobacco, I don't know. But she never got over it. She made collecting cigarette packs her mission. Every night she would go outside and gather them up from God knows where. But sure enough, when I would get up sometime in the morning, there on my front porch, and sometimes the back porch, too, would be several cigarette packs. Sometimes these packs would be empty, sometimes not. It was not unusual to find five or six each morning.

I figure this took her some time. First she had to find them, probably in a neighbor's garage or trash, and bring them back one by one. It must have taken her all night to cover both porches. Sometimes, in the middle of the night, I would hear her at the front door, making that "I've got a mouse" sound they make. I'd open the door, and there would be an excited Sweety, cigarette pack in her mouth. She would drop it at my feet with a little nod and go back to the hunt. No wonder she slept all day. She worked nights.

Sometimes I'd get up in the morning and be fresh out of smokes. I'd go to the porch and see if there were any there. Usually I would be

49

in luck, though they were never my brand. The only break in this routine came when one morning I found an unusual thing among the cigarette packs. I picked up the little plastic bag and examined it. It was an unopened fishing lure, with a coil of line attached. I figured this was her way of telling me she wanted more fish.

My neighbor, Marilyn, became one of Sweety's favorite targets. Marilyn used to leave her smokes on the dashboard of her Thunderbird with the window rolled down. Sweety would steal them all the time. I would find them and bring them back to her with my apologies. Marilyn got the idea that she could roll the window up about half way and this would stop Sweety's thieving. Well, one day Marilyn was in the drive-thru at the bank. As she was sitting in line, she reached for her cigarettes and she felt something soft. It was a dead mouse. I guess Sweety thought this was a pretty fair trade. She was a good cat.

Sweety lived to be almost twenty. She missed it by a month. But right up to the end, she collected cigarette packs for me. Even after I quit smoking, she kept it up. I didn't have the heart to tell her I quit. It was her job, and everyone wants to feel useful. She was a good cat.

The Coconut Man

I knew a guy who ate nothing but coconuts. His reason for this was that he believed they contained The Pure White Light. He was the skinniest person I ever saw, including pictures of prisoners from Andersonville or Auschwitz or Vogue. I could draw him, because all I can draw is stick figures.

One day I suggested that maybe he should try some rice and some milk and some Swiss cheese with his coconuts. They were white and maybe they contained The Pure White Light, too. He found this suggestion highly ridiculous, totally illogical, potentially dangerous and almost unworthy of a response. This was a spiritual issue and my suggestion was nothing less than ignorance and nothing short of heresy.

"Well, maybe there are foods that contain *other* colors of the spectrum that would be just as good. Carrots are pretty spiritual, not to mention red snapper," I said, hopefully. But he just glared. I think he wanted to hit me, but luckily he didn't. He never spoke another word to me.

I guess what bothered me the most was that anyone could eat just one kind of food all the time. I like lobster, but I don't want it three meals a day everyday for the rest of my life. Every once in a while I'd probably want a coconut. This guy just wanted coconuts and didn't mix it up with a lobster now and then. That's discipline for you, I guess.

I never saw the Coconut Man again. I suspect he just faded away, and that wouldn't have been a very time-consuming process for him. But I always sort of hoped that he discovered other colors he could eat and that he's sitting somewhere in a La-Z-Boy, with a gut, watching the playoffs and eating Cheetos because they contain The Pure Orange Light.

That's why I eat them.

The Day the Cats Took Over the World

On the 22 of April, 1959, the cats took over the world, but they didn't tell anybody about it. That was the genius of their plan. They went on just as they had for thousands of years, sleeping mostly.

The world was completely unaware of this change. They had seen sleeping cats before. But this sleep was different. It was the sleep of conquest, each subtle twitch the ecstasy of victory and power. But you could see it in their smiles.

There is nothing we can do now. They're everywhere. They have us completely surrounded. They're in our homes, our yards and under our beds playing with something we haven't been able to find for weeks. Resistance is useless.

They control everything from behind this big blue curtain in a garage somewhere in Milwaukee, pulling the levers and pushing the buttons that make the world more catish. We are puppets, mindlessly doing their bidding and changing their litter. "Here, kitty kitty kitty," we think we are saying. But is it really, "Yes, Master, I am yours to command?" Yeah, it's pretty creepy all right. You bet.

"Sure, that's easy to say," you tell me. "But where's the proof?"

That's the beauty of their plan, man. It's hard to prove. They're real sneaky. But haven't you ever wondered why NASA spends billions of dollars a year developing new cat toys? You think these advanced clumping litters were created by *humans*? You really believe that all the black budgets are for weapons and faster jets? Yeah, one-drop-a-month flea repellent just *happened*. And now they're cloning allergy-free cats so everyone can have one or two or fifty in their house. And how about the all the hundreds of exotic varieties of cat food? Prawn in White Wine Sauce, Lobster Bisque, Rack of Lamb with Wild Rice, Coho Salmon with Lemon Dill Sauce, Seafood Newberg. You think *people* thought these up? You think humans want to spend 40 billion dollars a year on food for their cats that's better than what they're eating? And I guess it's just *coincidence* that the CIA is bringing in hundreds of tons of Guatemalan catnip through Miami every Wednesday. Sure. I guess you also didn't notice that Socks virtually *lived* in the Oval Office? Or that NAACP really stands for the National Association for the

Advancement of Cat Purposes? Or that The Animal Planet is the most popular cable channel in the world? Or that Garfield is on the front page of the comics now?

Oh, yeah. And the giant cat face on Mars, that's just an optical illusion, right?

So far we're safe. The cats still need us to do all the menial stuff they can't do for themselves. But somewhere, probably in an underground bunker in New Mexico, they're working on something that will make us humans obsolete. You can bet on it. And when they finally get those thumbs, look out.

Kona Lowell

The Filipino Monkey Head

Some people are born successful. They've got everything. Some people are born without a frog's chance in snowball hell. My friend was born without a head. Unkind people would give him hats for his birthday. Or ties. Or sunglasses. But he was pretty philosophical about it.

When we were kids, he used to get teased a lot. They would say, "So what are you going to be when you grow up? The head of a big corporation?" And then they would all laugh. My friend just ignored them.

When he got older, he started saving his money for a wooden head. He finally ordered one from the Philippines, but it never looked quite right. Actually it looked a lot like one of those monkey heads they carve out of coconuts. And the straps chafed his armpits. I think he was pretty disappointed, seeing how he had saved for years for that head. But it was better than nothing.

I always tried to be a good friend to him and went out of my way to avoid certain phrases, like "heads up," "well, I guess I'll be headin' home" and "put a head on this." It wasn't much, I know, but it was the least I could do. I think he appreciated it.

Naturally Halloween was his favorite time of year. He would put a big coat on and carry his Filipino monkey head under his arm and everyone would say, "Great costume." Of course the next day he would just be that guy without a head again.

But my friend was determined not to let his handicap keep him from living a normal life. He got a job at an elegant French restaurant as head waiter, but people just couldn't get used to him putting the tray on top of his shoulders, even though it was very efficient and made perfectly good sense. Next he tried opening a headshop, but he freaked all of his customers out and sent most of them into recovery. It was at this time I lost track of him.

Several years later I got an unexpected package with a Jamaican postmark. Inside was a letter and something wrapped in newspaper. I opened the letter. Seems my friend had finally succeeded at being normal and was living the good life as headmaster of an exclusive school for the blind in Ocho Rios. He was married and had two lovely

54

children, both born with heads, something he was quite pleased about. He sent me a picture of himself and the family and I was happy to see that his wife was not only very pretty, but also had a head. He said she loved him for his mind and the fact that he had no head to keep it in didn't bother her one little bit. She was considerate as well and never used the excuse, "Not tonight, I have a headache" in deference to his condition but amazingly, to his great delight, always acknowledged him as "the head of the household." Women like that are hard to find. You bet.

I guess it just goes to show that anyone can fit in, even if they have to go all the way to Jamaica to do it. I miss my friend and plan to go for a visit during the Spring break. I think about him all the time now. Oh yeah, that thing wrapped in newspaper was the wooden Filipino monkey head thing. I've got it on my mantelpiece, so it's kind of hard *not* to think about him all the time. He had a note attached to it: *Won't be needing this anymore. You keep it. Or give it to some needy headless person. Or use it as a doorstop. I don't care. Thanks for avoiding the "H" word all those years. Your friend, Hedley.*

Parents can be so cruel.

The Girl with One Sad Eye

She's very pretty, like a model. Not a fashion model, but an artist's model. Subtle, like moss. Comfortable, like pie. It's hard to look at her, and harder not to. She looks like she should be backlit, photographed only in black and white. She has a matte finish, like acid free paper, crisp, pliable and faintly textured. She makes you want to feel her with your eyes closed, to taste her with your touch, to draw her, to paint her, to sculpt her without tools, but with lips and teeth and tongue.

Her toes curl as if she's stepping into the too cold ocean for the very first time. Her fingers make everything she grasps beg for eternity to begin right now.

Her hair is fully realized, drawn and redrawn until someone got it just right. It moves all by itself, creates its own wind, a charcoaled breeze with the faint aroma of bruised clover.

Her breasts are perfect. They define the word. There should be a picture of them in the dictionary next to the word *breasts*. There should be a picture of them in the dictionary next to the word *perfect*.

Her stomach is like a no man's land that soldiers would march onto to die, knowingly, willingly, happily.

Her legs don't rhyme with anything.

Her ass proves the existence of God.

But her eyes. They haunt me even now. I can see them, black, like wet onyx dropped in melting snow. They see me. They see through me, through the wall behind me and on forever. The left one has a tinge of amusement in it, like it's in on the joke. But the right one is just a little sad, like someone having a really good time that knows it's all about to end. Too soon.

A poet would know what to do. I just paint what I see. She has one sad eye.

The Liars Bar

I don't drink in private. I go to the neighborhood bar. This is because I heard that solitary drinking can lead to alcoholism. So I get drunk in public. Better to be on the safe side, I figure.

My neighborhood bar is very small, because it's a very small neighborhood, if you could even call it a neighborhood. It's more like a bunch of people that all live in the same general area. At night they come down the mountain to the bar and lie to each other.

It's not an exciting bar, but it's comfortable and they have my brand of liquor. And real good beer sausage. I know everyone's names, or at least the ones they're using right now. You never know for sure because they could be lying. No, you can bet on it.

Still, they're mostly good people and have their reasons. Not necessarily good reasons, just reasons. Some are trying to avoid the law, of course, but most are just trying to avoid their pasts. I guess they figure if you change your name, then it's like all that stuff happened to someone else. I am considering trying this myself when I have enough of a past to avoid. Right now I'm working on building one up. It takes some effort I can tell you.

Most of the people at the bar use only first names, and I'm pretty sure they aren't their real names. You know, the ones their mom and dad gave them. These are usually pretty colorful, like Cowboy or Dirt or Highway or Big Dog or Crazy Keala or Oz. There are also about six or seven Jims. Sure. Jim. Yeah, right.

The girls are even worse. There's no telling what their real names are, but they're nice to have around. They smell better, too. They usually have names like Jasmine or Lei or Sonja or Kat. They're not strippers, but if they decided to go into that line of work they'd have the name ready.

People at this bar enjoy philosophy, and most of them have one they're proud of. The most common is the *Government Is Corrupt So I'm Not Paying Taxes* philosophy. Next is the *Life Is So Weird* philosophy. This is the one I like the best. It covers a lot of ground and at times overlaps with the *Women Are No Good, Man* philosophy or the *What Goes Around Comes Around* philosophy. I hold to the *Hey, It Can Only Get Better* philosophy myself, so people generally like to tell me their troubles. It's like being a bartender except I have to pay for my drinks. And I don't get tips.

On Friday night there's a live band. All these old hippies come down out of the mountains and dance. They're like those Japanese soldiers you hear about that are stuck on an island and don't know that the war's over. They don't know what year it is, or they don't care, and dance like they're at Woodstock. That means they sort of flail around and spin in circles. They don't even stop when the band takes a break. Some have flowers in their hair, as if they were on their way to San Francisco but got lost. It's the closest thing to a time warp you can find. People say "groovy" and actually mean it. And no one even laughs at them.

It's at times like this that I realize we have a pretty great bar. I mean, you have all these hippies whirling around like dervishes, bikers playing pool, cowboys drinking beer with fishermen and telling each other lies like only cowboys and fishermen can tell, carpenters and lawyers discussing natural law, old Filipino coffee farmers and nurses doing shots, and the girls with the names like strippers flirting with everybody and no one has a problem with anyone else. No one cares how much money you make or what kind of car you drive. I don't remember the last time I saw a real fight. That's because we don't allow it. It's our bar, and you can't fight in it. If you do, you're 86ed, and then where would you go? It's like being exiled. Or a leper. An exiled leper.

I worry that maybe I spend too much time at my neighborhood bar. Not because I drink too much, but because I'm getting spoiled. I get to thinking the rest of the world is just like this. You know, friendly. It's not, but it should be. Some days I'll plan to drive right on by, go straight home, but my car just turns into the parking lot, like an old trail horse heading back to the barn. Before I know it, I'm talking to some cowboy named Bones about bluegrass and ghosts and Appaloosas and buffaloes and the beer and the lies are flowing and everything's right. You could even say groovy.

The Mailman of Memphis

The mailman left his bag on the porch, that's all. It was night so he just stopped. They don't deliver at night because there's too many stars and they can't concentrate on where the cracks in the sidewalk are. It's the light, you see. It distracts them.

I think he'll come back in the morning and get his mailbag, once the stars are gone and the sun comes up and it's safe again. At least relatively safe. The sun is a star, too, which can be just as distracting, but not as dangerous. Our mailman has no fear of the sun. He laughs at the sun. Rain, too, he disdains as but a weak and unworthy opponent, though insolent in demeanor.

His steel is sharper,
his blade more cunning,
more deftly wielded.

No plowman he, who knew full well and sure the temples of Karnak,
their secret rooms,
doorways hid beneath stone and sand and graven curses
spanning age to age.

He remains unfazed.
It is his job;
but more than that, his fate, to be the one that brings the news,
the good,
the ill,
to waiting ladies,
tepid coffee in their cups,
cups with kisses on the rims
and matching shades upon their lips.
But ware the dog! He bites!

For danger lurks at every turn,
and mortal life, though proud,
must yield and caution be the word that's by
and guards the chain link gate.

Kona Lowell

To enter here must more than mortal be,
or least be stout in Terror's face,
and calm the beating in his breast,
and tame that thumping harbinger of that which haunts dynastic
dreams,
the dreams that drift upon the Nile,
among the languid ibises that spurn the worm
and grasp the asp.

The Man Who Forgot His Name

I knew a man who forgot his name. It was Douglas. I would call up and say, "Hi. Is Douglas there?" And he would say, "No. There's nobody here by that name."

I saw him once in front of the bowling alley and said, "Hi, Douglas. What's up?" But he just ignored me and walked inside to go bowling, or maybe get a sandwich. I didn't go in because I didn't have any shoes.

Another time I went to the movies and guess who was sitting there big as life next to me? Douglas. "Hi, Douglas," I said.

"Will you stop bothering me?" he said. "My name's not Douglas."

"Well, sure it is. I've known you for 36 years."

"No you haven't."

"Well, sure I have."

"No you haven't. It's more like 37 years."

"Even better. 37 years. Okay. So what's up, Douglas?"

"My name's not Douglas."

"Well what is it then?"

"Alphonse."

"I think I would remember if your name was Alphonse. It doesn't sound anything like Douglas. I've always called you Douglas. For 36 years."

"37. And you were always wrong."

"Well, why didn't you correct me? Why didn't you tell me your name was Alphonse and not Douglas? Why did you let me call you Douglas for 36 or 37 years?"

"I didn't want to humiliate you. Besides, *your* name is Douglas."

"No way."

"Of course it is. I figured you knew that."

"Well that explains everything. Wow. Thanks a lot. Hey, what's this movie about anyway?"

"Well, there's this guy who's real simple-minded and eats chocolates, and he has all sorts of adventures and meets all these famous people. Then he goes to Viet Nam and runs real fast and ends up making a bunch of money selling shrimp or something."

"Oh yeah. Robert DeNiro's great."

"It's Tom Hanks."

"Really? I always thought that was Robert DeNiro."

"I know."

"Well why didn't you tell me that Tom Hanks wasn't Robert DeNiro?"

"I didn't want to humiliate you."

"Oh. Hey, thanks Douglas."

"Don't mention it."

The Mayberry of the Pacific

I live in a very small town on the island of Hawaii. It's so small it's really not a town at all. I like to think of it as the Mayberry of the Pacific, which it is, except that we have more than one town drunk.

Nothing much happens here, except parades. A parade can happen at the drop of a hat. Anybody's hat. I guess this is because Hawaiians are really into pageantry. Or it could be they just really like parades. Whatever the reason, they think nothing of bringing the entire town to a screeching halt to have one. Actually, "screeching" is probably not the right word. That would imply that things were really clipping along and then suddenly they weren't. It's more like getting your bicycle wheel stuck in the mud.

See we only have one highway, which is a two-lane blacktop, so if you need to get somewhere when a parade is going on you're just out of luck. It's not a good time to have a heart attack because you couldn't get to the hospital. But there's not much chance that any of our parades would ever induce a heart attack anyway. However, were the unthinkable to happen, the mortuary is conveniently located right next to the hospital (The rumors about a chute running directly from the hospital to the mortuary are untrue. I think.).

When most people envision a parade, they think of something like the Macy's Thanksgiving Day Parade or the Tournament of Roses Parade. These spectacular events require a year's planning, billions of dollars and thousands of people to pull them off. In my town, you can have a parade if you have at least two running cars, a hula dancer and some guy to throw hard candy at you.

The other night I was in a hurry to get home. There was a special, *The Incredible Secret World of Wombats,* on the Discovery Channel that promised to be highly enlightening as to these remarkable creatures' little understood behavior. But as I rounded the curve into town, I saw the traffic had stopped. This could be only mean an accident or a parade. Sure enough, as I crept down the road, I saw cars parked on all the shoulders and hundreds of people lining the street. Several boy scouts were huddled together under their flag and a hula *halau* was lining up in their colorful costumes. A racing canoe was atop a festively decorated (tinsel) wrecker (our version of a float) and several musicians were tuning up. This was going to be a big one.

Fortunately for me, the parade had not yet started so I was able to snake my way through eventually. But by the time I got home I had missed the special about wombats and never did find out exactly what secrets their world held or why they were incredible. Disappointed, I turned around and went back to town to catch the tail end of the parade. It was over, a few pieces of hard candy in the street being the only sign it had passed that way. I guess this was a lesson to me. As I sat on the curb sucking on a raspberry sourball, I realized that no matter how small the parade is, you should just stop and watch it.

The Man with Two Right Brains

Some people are born with two left feet. I was born with two right brains. I didn't figure this out by myself, of course. I have no left brain, so I couldn't. A brain doctor told me.

You see, I was sitting at my desk one day and my calculator went out. I don't know why, it just did. Probably something a left-brained person would get right away, but all I knew was that it didn't work anymore. The problem was, I had to do this thing where you divide one number by another. Every time I tried I got a different answer. So I went out and bought a new calculator.

That night, I stopped by the local bar for a beer and got to talking to this guy on the next stool. Turns out he was a doctor. "That's nice," I said when he told me. "What kind of doctor are you anyway?" I was hoping he was a vet because my cat had been acting distant lately. I don't remember the exact word he used but it ended up meaning "brain doctor."

We got to talking and I told him about my bum calculator and my math troubles. He suggested I come by his office the next day for some tests. "Will it hurt?" I asked. He said no, he wasn't going to open up my head or anything, just ask me some questions. "Good," I said, "I would hate to have to get my head shaved again. It looks pretty goofy when it's growing back out. I have a weird scalp."

The next day I went to his office. We got right to work. He had me do some doodling, fill out some forms and some other things I didn't quite understand. Then he asked me a lot of questions.

"If you found out that a nuclear strike had been launched and you were in the target area, what would you do?"

"Well, I would probably write a poem."

"Sure. Good. Now then, you're driving down the freeway and your car stalls miles from the nearest town. What do you do?"

"Well, I would probably finish this song I'm working on. I take my axe everywhere. You never know. I've got the whole thing down, but the hook right before the chorus is driving me crazy. It goes like this: nuh nuh dah, nuh nuh dah do do do. See what I mean? Then I'd hitch to Santa Fe for the Glass Blowing Festival."

"What about your car?"

"You said it was broken."

"Right. Okay. Which would you rather have for your birthday? A watercolor set or a new day planner?"

"What's a day planner?"

"Who do you admire more? Albert Einstein or Groucho Marx?"

"Groucho."

"Why?"

"Einstein's not that funny."

"He's not trying to be funny. He's a scientist."

"Then why does he look like a comedian?"

"What's 144 divided by 12?"

"Can I go get my calculator?"

"Sir, you have absolutely no left brain function whatever. How you have survived is a scientific wonder," he said to me. Then he put me in this contraption and took some pictures of my head. After he did this, he ran out of the room and got some other doctors to look at them. They kept looking at the pictures and looking at me. I started feeling sort of embarrassed.

They told me they wanted to do further studies because I was the only person they ever found with two right brains, but I said, "No, thanks. Go find someone else."

"But the odds of that would be 26,000,000,000,000 to 1. Do you know how long that would take?"

"No. Can I go get my calculator?"

Anyway, I felt pretty bad for a couple days, like I was some sort of freak or something. I wore a hat everywhere I went. But then I got to thinking it was really no big deal. I had done all right so far without a left brain. And I still can't see what having a left brain would do for me if I was about to be vaporized by a nuclear bomb, except that maybe I could figure out how long it would take to die without using a calculator. I think I'd rather be surprised.

The Monster Under My Bed

I always hated having that monster living under my bed. For one thing, he was difficult to vacuum around. "Move over and let me get that dust bunny," I'd tell him. He didn't like the vacuum cleaner one bit. I think it was the noise. He had sensitive hearing.

Another thing that really bothered me was getting into and out of bed. I always had to take sort of a flying leap to avoid getting my ankle grabbed. "Missed again," I'd say as I pulled the covers up over my head. He hated that. I mean it was basically his whole job and he really sucked at it.

He'd get back at me though. His favorite thing was stealing my shoes, but only one at a time. I would be late for school and have to wear two shoes that didn't match. It was embarrassing wearing one wingtip and one high top sneaker to class. And since I was already sort of on the fringe socially, this didn't spark a lot of party invitations.

He also seemed to enjoy annoying me when I was studying. Mom would say, "Time to do your homework." So I'd creep up to my room and sit at my desk, which meant my back was to the bed. This was not a good strategy, obviously, but there was no place else to put the desk. So I'd be writing a theme about *Silas Marner* or *Jane Eyre* and be trying to keep one eye on the bottom of the bed, just in case. The monster was too smart to show himself, but he'd do little things to irritate me, like clear his throat or hum a popular TV theme song. He knew it really bothered me.

Then something happened. We moved. Not just down the street, but clear across the whole country. I was thrilled. My new bedroom was all set up and I figured I was finally rid of that stupid monster. But that night when I turned off the light to go to sleep, I heard a familiar voice humming the theme song to *Leave It To Beaver*.

"Hey," I shouted. "What the hell are you doing here, you stupid monster? You weren't supposed to follow us all the way down here! Damn! I thought you were gone for good!"

There was total silence. Then I heard a faint sob coming from under the bed. Soon it was actual crying. It made my bed shake.

67

"Hey, look, I didn't really mean that," I said after some time. "It's okay. Just don't grab my ankles, all right?"

"Deal," he said.

After that, I never really had any more trouble. Oh, he would take the odd shoe now and then and hum at inappropriate times, but other than that he was okay for a monster and I figured if any one tried to clobber me in my sleep, they'd have to get past him first. So I slept pretty good.

I don't know what happened to him. When I came back from college one day, he was gone. I threw some shoes under the bed, but nothing happened. I asked my mom if she had moved anything out of my room but she said no, she had left everything just as it was, so she could remember me better. But she had noticed that one thing was missing. On my desk had been a picture of me, taken on my seventh birthday, sitting on a pony. It was gone.

"Yeah," I said. "I think a friend of mine took that."

The Sliding Door in Time

I had a sliding glass door on my house. It was in my kitchen. Supposedly it led to the back yard, but in reality it was a sliding door in time.

If you looked at it, it seemed to be a normal sliding glass door, somewhat dirty and covered with fingerprints, and one prominent forehead print.

Most people never realized this door led to another time. They would sit in my kitchen, drink coffee and look out through the glass door at my back yard. There was a little patio out there with a lone pot of geraniums, a wooden fence, minus a slat or two, a sprinkler and an old dog bowl. I had planned to get a dog, but never got around to it.

I never told them this was a door to another time. But every once in a while someone would go outside. Then they would find out for themselves. I would just smile when they came back in and wait for them to tell me what happened. I would usually have to say, "I live here, you know. I know all about it." But I would listen anyway. I could see why they might be excited.

I never did figure out exactly what time it was out there, but I guess it must have been quite long ago, because it was sort of a swamp, with ferns about 20 feet tall. Sometimes when I had leftovers, I would put them out back for the dinosaurs. They seemed to especially enjoy day-old spaghetti, at least the little ones did anyway. They're real cute when they're puppies.

I enjoyed sitting in the swamp. I would take the newspaper out back and sit on an old fallen fern trunk and read the personals and the box scores. This also served as some protection because if the dinosaurs got too pushy I could whack them on the nose with the rolled up newspaper. It didn't hurt them, but they didn't like it too much.

Then one day it all came to an end. There's a reason why your mother always said, "Don't throw the ball in the house." When my new sliding door was installed, I held my breath and opened it. But it just led to the patio with the geranium. I opened and closed it several more times but it was now the correct time. It still is. But once in a while I put some leftover spaghetti out there just in case.

Kona Lowell

The Spirit of Fontenessi

The spirit of Fontenessi hovered like frozen breath
suspended, not moving, still and translucent
in the chill late autumn dusk beneath the cypress trees.

He was searching for something he had left behind.
Something he had forgotten.
Something he could not forget.
Distant, vague like a shadow cast by an old photograph.

He dripped on the cold stone.
He blew softly on the brown grass.
He grazed the plastic flowers with incapable fingers.

"Where are you?" he asked. No answer. Hush.

The spirit of Fontenessi hovered like a prayer
rose-scented and earnest in the failing light
of the still late autumn dusk beneath the cypress trees.

"Where are you?" he asked. No answer. Hush.

He clawed the frozen ground.
He flew around the stone.
He spiraled into the memories piled on the lawn
like careless pirate treasure.

The spirit of Fontenessi hovered like a thought
captive and restless, fixed like a bayonet
in the chill late autumn dusk beneath the cypress trees.

"Where are you?" he asked.

"Where I have always been. Hush."

The spirit of Fontenessi went home.
It was in his pocket all the time.

70

The Stream of Consciousness

I used to have an old shack in the woods. The woods were older than the shack, and through the middle of them, and right next to the shack, ran the Stream of Consciousness.

On Sunday mornings I would go fishing in the Stream of Consciousness. Usually I would catch enough fish to make a fine Sunday fish fry. This might have been because of my lucky hat or because there were thousands of fish in the stream. I never found out, because I always wore my lucky hat.

The fish from the stream were especially tasty and unusual. Eating them would suddenly remind me of the fish my mother used to cook when we would stay at this little lake cabin up in Michigan. We ate them faster than she could fry them up. I had to take a bath in the kitchen sink. The air smelled like pine and sand and seagulls and the green water of Lake Michigan. The blueberries there were just delicious, especially in pancakes. But no pancakes can compare to the cherry pancakes they make in Traverse City. It's really beautiful there when all the cherry trees are in bloom. Like Japan. I went there for the Cherry Blossom Festival to sell pancakes and met this really pretty girl in a discotheque. She was as slim as my chances. She wasn't interested in dancing, but her lips were remarkable, like red satin pillows. We both liked fish so I took her out for a fish dinner. We sat on the floor on pillows. It was good, but not as good as the fish I used to catch in the Stream of Consciousness.

One Sunday morning as I was fishing, I sort of dozed off. Fishing will do that to you. Before I knew it, I slid into the stream. My whole life, from my first childhood memory to watching the bobber on the water five seconds earlier, raced through my mind like a VCR stuck on fast forward. I came to sputtering and coughing and dragged myself back on to the bank. "Whew!" I said aloud. "That was close."

It was then I decided that, lucky hat or not, I had better fish someplace else where I could fall asleep without the danger of reliving my entire life at high speed. Still, I do miss the fish. And Michigan. And Japan. And the girl with lips like red satin pillows.

The Very Bad Grocery Store

I shop at a very bad grocery store. I don't have any choice. It's the only one near my house, just down below me on the mountain. The people who run it are not bad, just inept. I think their previous business experience was having a garage sale.

They seem to have no concept of this thing called "stocking" where you fill up shelves with several of the same item and arrange them in a logical order. They have whole shelves that are empty and some that are full of hundreds of packages of dried squid. It's like someone just drives up in a truck and says, "Hey, how about 500 packages of dried squid?" and they say, "Sure, why not?" In the meantime they're out of cereal and bread. But if you're looking for dried squid you've hit the mother lode.

The store seems to have been arranged by explosion. The diapers are next to the cat food. The bread and peanut butter are on opposite ends of the store. The cows tongues are next to the pigs feet, which is correct and therefore accidental. The Mexican food has been segregated on an island of its own, except for various products that have somehow emigrated to random sections of the store and are now hiding out from the authorities.

One time I asked the manager to get me something. They used to have this frozen yogurt I liked. Then they ran out. I told him I really liked this brand and to please get some more. "Sure," he said. The next time I came in they had three new brands where mine used to be. So I figured I better quit before they got rid of something else I liked.

The store gets pretty busy. To keep it nice and full of customers, they like to put a teenager on the main register. Next to him is a sign that says, "NO TOBACCO OR ALCOHOL. MINOR ON DUTY." Of course everybody has tobacco or alcohol so they all have to go to the other register while he sits there folding bags and picking his nose. Most people have finished their alcohol by the time they leave.

For some time now they have threatened to open a deli in the store. The glass counters have been there about a year. The other day they had food in the counters, but no one behind them. So I went and asked the cashier if I could get some potato salad from the deli. She said no, the deli was closed now. I asked her when it was going to be open but she didn't know. I figured I better not press my luck or they'd take the deli out entirely.

Even though this is a very bad grocery store, I must say that they have excellent sackers, if you ever make it that far. I mean these guys really do it right. They wrap paper bags around things, put rubber bands on them and double bag others and it's really impressive, sort of like going to Benny Hanna's and watching them cook, except it's putting groceries in bags. Sometimes we clap when they're done.

Then we go home and eat our dried squid.

The Tuesday Before the Big Bang

The Tuesday before the Big Bang was pretty much like every other Tuesday that had come before it. Every Tuesday was pretty much like every Monday, Wednesday, Thursday, Friday, Saturday and Sunday for that matter. But this Tuesday would prove to be slightly different.

God was planning a surprise birthday party for Gabriel. He wanted the place to be festive so He got some paper lanterns and streamers and some balloons. "I've got to bake a cake for Gabriel's birthday," He said to His Son. "Get someone to hang up the paper lanterns and the streamers. You take this bag of balloons and blow them all up." Then He went into the kitchen to bake the cake.

A few minutes later He came back out, stirring a big bowl of batter. "Oh yeah," He said, "We also need a banner that says *Happy Birthday Gabriel* on it. Get someone to make one, but for heaven's sake don't let Gabriel know! This is supposed to be a surprise."

His Son got Michael to make the banner because Michael had sort of a flair for those kind of things. He gave Michael a big roll of white shelf paper and a blue Marks-A-Lot. A few minutes later His Father came back out, licking a large wooden mixing spoon covered with icing. "By the way," He said, "don't blow those balloons up too full. We don't want them to explode."

"Why not?" His Son asked.

"Because it could create a universe. We've got enough to do without having a universe to look after. Oh, there's the timer! I have to check on my cake."

But God's Son did not know His own strength and a few minutes later, at 11:59 pm, there was a loud explosion. God came out of the kitchen, covered with flour, His hands on His hips. "What did I tell You?" He said. "Now You've gone and created a universe. Well, You've always wanted a pet, now You've got one. But You have to take care of it Yourself. Don't ask Me to feed it. It's Your responsibility."

"Sorry, Dad."

"The worst thing is You made My cake fall. Now I have to start all over again."

"Sorry, Dad."

"Sorry doesn't bake cakes, Son."

And that was the Tuesday before the Big Bang. The party came off splendidly. Gabriel was completely surprised and the cake was delicious. Everyone had a great time, in spite of the new universe growing outside, except Michael who was a bit embarrassed for having misspelled "Birthday" on the banner.

Things I Never Knew

I never knew how pretty you were until I saw you with someone I really hated and wanted to kill, slowly and painfully and in a creatively malevolent way, like a Bond villain with a high-pitched voice and creepy eyebrows wearing a Nehru jacket and surrounded by indifferently beautiful women of dubious morals and deadly kung fu skills.

I never knew I had limitations until my head hit the ceiling with a resounding "thump."

I never knew Frank Sinatra, but I remember a song his daughter used to sing about boots.

I never knew so many people had dogs with last names.

I never knew enough to make me dangerous or rich.

I never knew I would miss you before you left and would want you to leave again so I could miss you some more and get over it.

I never knew my laugh was funnier than what I was laughing at.

I never knew that sheep could go for days without dreaming.

I never knew that the Farmer's Almanac was a book farmers used. I just thought it was written by some guy named Farmer.

I never knew soup was considered real food worldwide.

I never knew that chameleons could give birth whenever they felt like it.

I never knew I wasn't adopted.

I never knew dancing could lead to even more dancing.

I never knew the meaning of wife.

I never knew that a pretty girl was like a melody. I thought it was "malady."

I never knew the way to San Jose.

I never knew a man I didn't like, but I met plenty.

I never knew a secret someone else didn't already know.

I never knew you cared.

Late Thursday Night at the Bamboo Cafe

She's like a windowless room.
No doors, either.
Cold as reason, silent as thought.
No way in, no way out.

Remote, like a gum wrapper left on the moon,
I wait for her to notice. Please.

Here I am. Look. It's me, you know, *me*.

She can't see me.
There are no windows, no doors.
Hard as science, brittle as religion.
No way out, no way in.

Still, she's beautiful,
like an ice carving of a naked, leafless willow
or a frozen lake with one silent swan
patiently waiting for the Spring thaw. Hurry. Please hurry.

Here I am. Look. I'm right here.

But she can't see me.
There are films in the way, and books.
Boyfriends that left her sitting by the phone
while they did something else, or gave up, or ran away.
Caution turned into career, anger became style,
tears became stone and broke the cold tile of the bathroom floor.

Now she's encased, cocooned, as impenetrable as myth,
armored by memory, steel-plated with doubt, fear
and the certainty that it's dangerous out there.

She can't see me.
There are no windows, no doors.
Not even a keyhole to peep through.

Still, she's very beautiful.

Maybe I should just say hi.

Spider Boy

No one ever knew the Spider Boy. He didn't fit. It might have been his hair, which hung down over his forehead in a Will Rogersesque insolent flap, keeping him from ever being truly debonair. It might have been his fingers, too nimble for ordinary work, too delicate for labor, more suited to the harp than the hammer. It might have been his eyes, green like leaves with the sun shining through them, green like moss, too aware. Dangerous. He didn't fit.

The Spider Boy lived in the midst of New York City. He hid his talents there, binding them to the few trees that grew from the ashen pavement near the Algonquin Hotel with found string and twine. In the spring birds would steal the string for nests and he would have to start all over again.

The Spider Boy could sing, but not very well.

The Spider Boy could tie a knot like a 70 year old Malaysian sailor, except quicker. This was his gift. String, rope, twine – anything that could be tied or knotted, he could turn into something amazing, something that no longer resembled string or rope or twine. But no one cared. No one knew.

In the winter, alone in his room, he would invent new knots, elegant creations of pure mathematical brilliance, eternity in twine, endlessness in string. Each one he would hang on the wall, not as a trophy, but as a reminder. He kept no clock.

It's what he did. It's all he did. And as the years turned into decades and the building crumbled noiselessly, inch by inch around him, he tied more knots. Knots that could not be deciphered. Knots that couldn't be untied. Secret knots. Lovely knots. Painful knots. Knots that hinted at forgotten worlds where in another time he might have found a place to fit. A place where a Spider Boy would be welcomed, even honored. Cherished.

When the ambulance came to remove the Spider Boy, the EMTs were silent. They surveyed the tiny, dark room in quiet awe, not sure what it meant. The thousands and thousands of amazing knots hung in solid sheets, like huge, raveling tapestries, masking every surface until no wall could be seen. They looked at each other and shook their heads, gently lifting the Spider Boy onto the gurney. He was very light. There was not much left of him now. He was never very big anyway.

"What's that in his hands?" the one asked the other.

"It's string," his partner replied.

"I know that, but what is it?"

"Oh. It's that game. You know, cat in the cradle."

"Yeah. I remember that. My grandfather used to play that with me."

"Me, too. I forgot about that."

"But it takes two people to play it, right?"

"Yeah. Two."

Later

Later
when everyone goes home

Later
when there's nothing on TV

Later
when it stops raining

Later
when the cat's asleep

Later
when the moon is just right

Later
when we stop arguing

Later
when we make up again

Later
when I figure out exactly how to say it

I'll tell you that I love you

Too late.

Ere I Saw Elba

I always know
or think I do
the things you think
or think you do

as if I were a seer enisled
but with a vision measureless
compelled to see beyond the blue
that rings me in this rocky nest
and holds me here against my will.

That sail upon the edge of things
that keeps the sky and ocean two
might not in fact be sail at all
but distant hope in tactile form
imagined for my agony
a torture conjured for my crime
of seeing things the way I do
and knowing what I shouldn't know.

But you marooned me on this rock
you exiled me for lawlessness
and now you wish I would confess
to every subtle felony
(yes, yes, I do confess, I'm guilty, yes)
and every rule I did transgress
in what was youth's stupidity
and simple acts of carelessness.

But there's no need for cruelty.
I've suffered long, this sight's a curse
I'd give it back and sink into simplicity
without a single backward glance
or longing to reverse the course
that leads me to benightedness,
that dark and cozy womb I left

against all sense to take the chance
that knowledge was the same as bliss.

For sailors, those who journey far
and touch no land as seasons change,
would trade it all:
their insight gained in far-flung ports
where liquor's cheap and faces strange,
for just one kiss that's really meant
and just one night with one true love
who needs no proof, no testament,
but loves them just for who they are.

Rooster & Papaya

There is a young wild rooster that likes to visit my house in the early morning and practice his crowing. He is not very good at it yet. Instead of the typical cock-a-doodle-doo thing he does sort of a cock-ork-ack-urrrgh. It's pretty pathetic. I can do a better rooster impersonation. Anybody could.

The other problem is he doesn't have a very clear idea of when roosters are supposed to perform this basic function for which they're celebrated. A full moon is as good as a sunrise to him. Or a particularly bright star. Or a porch light. Or high beams on a truck coming up the mountain. A bright idea would probably set him off.

When you put this all together you get a rooster who is not making friends. Sometimes I'll have a late night at the Liar's Bar, shooting Chinese snooker and drinking Tennessee whiskey with the twin Srisai sisters from Patong Beach, and just be starting to fall asleep when I hear him practicing outside my window. I have never owned a gun, for a variety of reasons, but he is beginning to change my mind on this issue. I lie there imagining him disappearing in a puff of black and orange feathers as the shotgun goes off. Then I lie there feeling terrible because I never like to kill little critters of any kind, however annoying (or deserving). I stick an earplug in my ear and try to go back to sleep. My dreams are troubled by bloody visions of Foghorn Leghorn.

I just don't like to kill things. See, I have what's called a *hale 'au'au*, a Hawaiian shower room outside my house. The local rats figured this was a good place to party at night. I did not agree with them and told them so. They didn't listen. So I got a big rat trap at the hardware store. But my girlfriend (and me, too) found the results so unpleasant we ended up getting one of those sonic rat annoyers instead. It actually works and I don't have to deal with dead rats the size of kittens. Unfortunately, the man at the hardware store said they don't make them for roosters. But he did have a nice shotgun.

I told a local friend of mine about the problem with the rooster. He didn't quite understand my reluctance to "just shoot da buggah" and gave me a great Hawaiian recipe for rooster. Apparently cooking it with papayas makes it nice and tender. I guess he figured that if I knew it would taste really, really good, it would be easier for me to kill it. I thanked him for the recipe but didn't bother to tell him that my experience with preparing dead animals for eating was limited to fish.

So the rooster is still there. His crowing hasn't improved. But lately he has been practicing out in the jungle so my sleep has been relatively undisturbed. This morning, as I drank my coffee on the front porch, he made his way through my yard, pausing to look at me before going about his own business. He is actually a very beautiful bird, extremely colorful, with long, shiny tail feathers and a bright red comb and wattles. Hopefully he'll move on to some other place where there's lonely hens who will appreciate him, lousy crowing or not. Meanwhile, I'm keeping the rooster and papaya recipe on the refrigerator door.

Pig and Duck

Pig was exceedingly upset. In times like these, times of great desperation and moment, she would usually consult the wisest animal (other than herself) that she could find, but today her selection was extremely limited. Only Duck was available, lurking about the barnyard, pecking here and there at what might or might not be bugs.

Pig liked Duck, as much as anyone of superior intellect possibly could, but never confided in her. Their relationship consisted of polite "Good mornings" and the occasional courteous "Excuse me, I was going to sit in that puddle." Today, though neither of them suspected a thing, all of that was about to change – forever.

"Good morning, Duck," Pig said, as she approached.

Duck looked up with a bill full of mud, still chewing something, and responded with, "Good morning, Pig. You look well today." But secretly Duck detected a hint of sadness, or perhaps, she thought, "wistfulness," in Pig's demeanor. "Is everything alright?" she asked.

"Well, now that you mention it, and thank you for asking, no," Pig answered somewhat stiffly. "That is, yes and no. I have a slight problem and I just don't know how best to deal with it."

"Well you know Pig, I would be very happy to help in anyway that I can," Duck returned kindly. "You aren't ill, are you?"

"No, no. Nothing of the sort. It's just that, well, I just don't feel fulfilled, if you know what I mean."

"Ah," Duck replied, "I know that feeling. I can eat twenty or thirty June bugs and I'm still hungry."

"No," Pig answered patiently, "not *that* kind of fulfilled. I meant that I don't feel fulfilled in my *life*. There's something I desperately want, something I dream of day and night, but…"

"But you are afraid to defy convention and just reach out and grab your destiny by the throat?"

Pig looked at Duck in wonder. "Exactly!" she said.

"So what is this dream?" inquired Duck.

"You won't laugh?" Pig asked meekly.

"Of course not, dear girl."

"Well, I always wanted, I mean I dream of being…"

"Yes?"

"A dancer! I want to dance, Duck, to dance! To float about the stage to the romantic strains of Tchaikovsky, the frenetic eroticism of Stravinsky and the folksy charm of Copland! To dance, Duck, on these pointed hooves, spinning and leaping as no pig has ever done, to the deafening applause of my loyal and devoted fans, an earsplitting hurricane of appreciation, softened only by the hundreds of red roses tossed upon the stage as I curtsy and smile."

"That's beautiful," said Duck. "Simply beautiful. I too have a dream, but I have never dared breathe it to a living soul, that is, until this very moment. You see, Pig, I dream of being a great singer, to fill the furthest, highest corner of the Met with my beautiful, soaring voice, to gloriously trill the exotic *Aida*, to live the role of Elvira, to revel in the playfulness of *Cosi fan tutte* or the intrigue of *La Flute Enchante* as my adoring fans weep at the mere thought of my heavenly voice!"

There was silence. Pig and Duck looked at each other. They saw no more Pig and Duck, but two kindred spirits, two sisters of the soul, with dreams too big for their barnyard.

"What shall we do?" Pig asked.

"There's only one thing *to* do," said Duck. "Catch the next train for New York City."

And that was that. Pig and Duck were never seen at the farm again. The Metropolitan Opera never toured such small towns and the Ballet Russe was of course always on a hectic European schedule.

Unwilling Immigrants

They never asked to be here, to be dragged from their homes and families in Africa. Their layover in Jamaica was not a vacation, their quarters there no resort. They had no choice. Now they're here. It's too late to go home.

There are no records, no genealogy kept in musty files, no plaques on Ellis Island commemorating their arrival. They were brought here to work. That's all. Many of them never even made it here, dying at sea, cramped together in unfit and squalid conditions.

They have suffered every indignity, been killed like vermin and blamed for things they didn't do. They have always been the scapegoats for whatever is wrong. "They breed like rabbits," people say. "They destroy everything," they say. "The only good one is a dead one," they say.

Still they try to band together, to raise their families and live their lives. But it's tough when everyone hates you just because of what you are. You can't change that, or where you're from. It's hard being a mongoose in Hawaii.

The Importance of Being Ernesto

"You see," he told me one day when I had inadvertently called him Ernest for the second or third time, "Ernests abound."

I waited for him to continue with this thought, but I guess he felt that enough had been said. I settled back into my own meditations. How could the huge stones of the pyramids be brought to the Giza Plateau on wooden rollers if there were no trees to make the wooden rollers from?

"Ernesto, on the other hand, defies convention. It is a celebratory name, even heroic."

"Excuse me?" I replied, startled from my reverie by this new concept.

"I said that Ernesto is a name filled with drama, an epic name. A conquistador might be named Ernesto," he said with a faraway look, sort of like a senior class picture.

"Well, Che Guevara's real name was Ernesto. I guess it could have held him back if everyone had called him Ernest," I replied, thinking I had finally caught his drift.

"My point exactly! A name fit for a conquistador, or a revolutionary!" he responded with a slight accent I had never noticed before.

"But Guevara was a Latino. He was born in Argentina. You have red hair."

"There were conquistadors with red hair," he answered with some dignity, his accent becoming more pronounced.

"Well, maybe. But there's nothing wrong with the name Ernest. Hemingway didn't do too bad with it," I countered.

"Si. Si. That's why he had everyone call him *Papa!*" he shouted, his sudden Spanish accent becoming nearly impenetrable.

"Okay, okay. Well what about Ernest Borgnine then?"

"You mean the guy on *McHales Navy*? You would compare him to a conquistador? He's *fat!*" he screamed, his Rs rolling uncontrollably.

"You aren't exactly skinny. Anyway, Borgnine did a lot more than *McHales Navy*. He won the Oscar for *Marty*. He was in all sorts of great movies."

"Si, si. And this Señor Marty, what was his, how you say, job, in this movie, eh? Que? Que?"

"He was a butcher."

"Aha! And you would have the *cajones* to compare a butcher to a conquistador?" he thundered.

"Yes."

"Do you want to deliver this pizza, or do you want me to do it?"

"You go ahead, Ernesto."

"Gracias."

So You Want to Be a Writer

Everybody thinks writing is easy. It isn't. Oh, I know it's not physically demanding, like being a bull wrestler, tuna fisherman or fashion model, but it's still not a day at the beach, unless you write at the beach.

People imagine a writer's life to be glamorous and exciting. Maybe it is, if your idea of glamour is me in my underwear, unshaved, eating Cheetos, and you equate excitement with word processing. I know, Hemingway did all sorts of glamorous, exciting things, like bull fighting and deep sea fishing and big game safaris in Africa. But when he was writing *The Sun Also Rises* he was just sitting there in his underwear eating Cheetos. In fact Hemingway's life was so damn exciting he just couldn't wait for it to be over.

But things have changed in the exciting world we writers inhabit. In the old days, you got what was called "writer's cramp." This was a painful ailment caused by continuously erasing with a pencil. Now we get carpal tunnel syndrome from continually backspacing and hitting Control Alt Delete.

If this were not bad enough, and it is, there is also the mysterious little muse assassin called "writer's block." This evil and mischievous imp can strike at any time, literally draining every ounce of creative fluid from the brain, or as we writers call it, "the idea factory." When this happens, there's nothing left but Hollywood.

The other drawback to a literary career that no one ever considers is the fact that writers don't get the women. Musicians get them. Race car drivers get them. Actors get them. Football players get them. All these guys get harems of gorgeous women, all of them on loan from Victoria's Secret, with names like Bambi and Danielle and Jennifer. Writers get women in glasses with names like Zelda and George.

Maybe you think I'm kidding about the woman thing. Try this sometime. Walk into a gathering of babes (I don't know where they gather, I'm a writer) and say, "Hi there. I just finished my exhaustive biography of H. L. Menken. It took seven years and critics say it is *the* definitive volume on Menken's life and work." See how many of them rip their tops off. Now say, "Hi there. I got Russell Crowe's spit in my hair." You won't be able to walk for days.

But I don't want to give the impression that there are no benefits to being a writer. That would be unfair. First of all, you get really, really immune to rejection. It's like an inoculation every day. Second, you get to be your own boss, unless you count the publisher, the editor and your agent, but since you'll almost never hear from them anyway, you're pretty much on your own. Third, there's no overhead. You can write anywhere on almost anything, though eventually you must transfer your writing from napkins, business cards and burger wrappers to a more conventional medium. Fourth, ideas are free. Of course, so are fish, if you can catch them. Fifth, and this is probably the greatest thing, writers become immortal. Long after you're gone, your work forgotten and unread, people will be using your name in the *Sunday New York Times* crossword puzzle for a really tough clue. Like this: Erstwhile Boston poet laureate on Hawaii's leeward coast.

Okay, okay, look at my damn name. It's on the cover of the book.

At the End of the Day

There are phrases in the English language that are timeless and endearing, like "cuter than a box full o' spaniel pups" or "I'll slap you like a red-headed stepchild." There are phrases that are also wholly American and sort of quaint, and therefore reassuring, like "I do not choose to run," "I am not a crook" and "I did not have sex with that woman." But there are also phrases, many of which become far too popular, that are irritating beyond endurance. The worst of these is, "At the end of the day."

It is now virtually impossible to listen to an interview, especially in the political arena, without someone using this obnoxious expression at least a dozen times. And what does it mean? Who knows? I used to believe that "Just do it!" or maybe "Where's the beef?" were the worst, but I've changed my mind. This ridiculous idiom has so insidiously permeated our culture that now even foreign dignitaries, people who can barely put a complete sentence together in English, work this one in. I guess it's their way of proving they understand us. Or their way of laughing at us.

It is mind numbing how government spokespersons will apply this little gem of a catchphrase. Let's say some suit is speaking about human rights violations in China. He will say, with the straightest of faces, "It is incumbent on the Chinese government, at the end of the day, to stop brutally torturing college students who peacefully oppose their harsh leadership." Really? Do they actually need to wait until the end of the day to enact this policy? Does it mean that it is only incumbent on them at sunset? Reform is a specifically "evening" sort of thing? It would make as much sense to say, "It is incumbent on the Chinese government, who are cuter than a box full o' spaniel pups, to stop brutally torturing college students who peacefully oppose their harsh leadership."

Sadly, there's nothing we can do, because this phrase is now an accepted part of the collective consciousness of the entire country, like rap or pierced navels. We just have to ride it out and hope that someone will craft another expression to replace it. In the meantime, the Lakers' bench is just too deep at the end of the day, so I suggest playing them in the morning. Or in the afternoon. And somewhere around suppertime the races must learn to live together in harmony. And just before bed we must do something about nuclear proliferation. That leaves us the entire night and most of the morning free to just do it.

The Rain House

It always rains there. That's why everything is green, hundreds of shades of green, from the palest chartreuse to the deepest forest green, a green that is just this side of black. The stones are green with moss. So are the trunks of the trees, even their branches and twigs. There are green birds in them and they make their nests from green grass.

I went there years ago and stayed for several days. My shoes started turning green, as did my pants and shirt, as if they were ashamed to be the only things not green in this completely green place. My eyes are green, but when I came home they were even greener, still reflecting the leaves and the trees and the birds.

Did I mention that it rains? I don't know where all the water goes, why the whole world is not under water by now. I prowled through this liquid green realm for days, up green paths and down, into ancient untrodden hollows and up onto sharp ridges like the backs of sleeping green dinosaurs. It was impossible to light a fire. Lightning could not set this jungle on fire. Only at night did it stop being green. It was totally dark, like being buried alive. But I could still tell it was green all around me. I could smell green. I could feel green. I dreamed green dreams. The rain came down in one long song.

One morning I woke in the endless rain and decided to hike to the next ridge. I couldn't see very far because of the trees and the rain. As I reached the top of the ridge, I looked down below my feet into a deep, green, bowl-shaped valley bisected by a swift moving stream. There in the center, just on the other side of the stream, stood a small shack. Smoke came from the old rusty chimney and fought the insistent rain in a hopeless battle. But I would never have noticed the shack without the smoke. I couldn't imagine that anyone could actually live down there, so far from everything, in so much green. I climbed warily down the slippery green path, grasping the slick, green branches that luckily overlapped it every few feet.

The stream, though swift and cold, was only knee-deep and I waded across easily. There were small green fish in pockets of calm water near the bank. But if it were not for the smoke, I would have thought the house was deserted. It was almost entirely covered in vines, with ferns sprouting here and there from parts of the nearly hidden, rusty roof, the grass chest-high and almost impenetrable around its rotting lanai.

I wasn't sure what to do, but I was tired of the rain and the thought of being dry, with a warm, friendly fire, overpowered my natural shyness and reluctance to put myself in an awkward position. I climbed the decaying, moss-covered wooden steps, and knocked tentatively on the old door, rainwater dripping on my shoulders through the gaping roof of the sagging lanai. Night was coming on.

Before I could reconsider and hurry away, the door opened. There, smiling at me, was a young Hawaiian woman in a leaf-green sarong, her black hair cascading almost to her bare, brown feet, and surmounted by a *lei palapalai,* a fern lei.

"*E komo mai i loko,*" she said in a voice more like music than speech. "Please come inside out of the rain."

Thanking her, I sheepishly entered the warm, dry room, the only light coming from the fireplace and several strategic candles. I could still hear the rain outside, but the vine-covered roof deadened the sound inside. She closed the door and it was still, silent and warm.

"Sit by the fire and warm yourself," she said, waving me to a cane chair, while taking my dripping rain gear. "I'll get you some hot tea."

"Thanks," I said. "Sorry to bother you, but I've been hiking through the rain for days and when I saw the smoke from your chimney I just couldn't help myself."

"Yes, it always rains here," she replied. "I was expecting you two days ago, but you went up the other ridge instead."

"You were expecting me?" I asked with some surprise.

"Of course. Here, drink this tea. It will warm you up while I cook dinner."

I have stayed in some of the finest hotels in the world, but at this moment I could not have imagined a more luxurious place to be. After days in the constant rain it was beyond nirvana to sit by a crackling fire, drink hot tea and be dry and warm again. I was starting to nod off when my hostess returned with a plate of fish, poi and rice. To this day, no food has ever compared with that simple meal.

When I had finished eating, the beautiful young woman sat down next to me on the dark-stained wooden floor, her hair spreading around her like black wings, and held her hands to the fire, warming them. "You know," I said, "I was so happy to be dry and you've been so kind and all that I forgot to even ask your name."

"You can call me Ua," she replied.

"I'm very happy to meet you, Ua. By the way, why'd you say you knew I was coming here? Did you see me on the other ridge?"

"No. I just knew. People always come here when they've been in the rain for too many days. It always rains here. That's why this place is called *Hale Ua*, the Rain House."

"Well I sure am glad you're here. I don't think I could have taken much more of that."

"Stay here tonight, and in the morning you'll feel better. It will make your journey back out of the valley easier," Ua said. Without another word she led me to a small cozy bedroom that held a tall wooden bed covered with an old Hawaiian quilt. I thanked her, snuggled under the covers, and was almost immediately fast asleep.

I woke sometime in the early morning, and looking outside saw the rain still falling in the green valley and dripping from the eaves above the window. I got out of bed more refreshed than I had felt in years. Going into the main room, I saw no sign of Ua. I called throughout the little house but got no answer. She must have gone out, I figured, though I couldn't imagine where to. I was glad to see, however, that she had left breakfast on the old table. There were papayas, rice, fish and sliced taro. I ate like a starving man.

After I finished breakfast, I went out on the lanai to have a smoke. There was still no sign of Ua. I figured that I should just leave, that maybe this was her way of saying goodbye, so I went back in and wrote a short thank you note and left it on the table. I slung my pack on my back and headed out, crossing the little stream and climbing slowly back up the slippery green path I had descended the day before. All the way up, the rain blew in my face as I struggled to reach the ends of the branches, hanging down like rescuing hands, to pull myself safely to the top. When I neared the summit, the rain slackened and when I reached the top it stopped altogether.

It felt eerie somehow, to stand on that sharp ridge, surrounded by a hundred different shades of green, and feel no rain. It always rains there. I turned and looked down into the valley and watched the sheet of rain that had just deserted me pull back like a waving curtain towards *Hale Ua*, the thin column of smoke still rising from its rusty chimney. But as the gray edge of the rain curtain drifted across the stream and touched the little shack, I rubbed my eyes. Where it had stood only moments before there was now only green and more green on either side of the stream. The smoke was gone and the chimney with it.

I couldn't stand it. I began to make my way back down the slippery path, but immediately fell and slid several feet. I got up and tried again with the same result, ending up muddy and scratched and grass-stained. As I sat there in my desperate confusion on the wet ground, I watched the rain curtain slowly moving back towards me from the other side of the valley. As it crossed the little stream, a rusty chimney suddenly stood out from the green behind it, smoke rising in a thin column against the unrelenting rain. Soon the rain reached the ridge on which I was standing, falling in a steady, Polynesian tattoo on all the hundreds of shades of green. It always rains there.

The Solid Green Birthday

I had a solid green birthday. I saw it coming.

"This looks like trouble," I said to no one in particular, but still not loud enough to alarm anyone.

I came home as if nothing was up. I played along, not wanting to spoil things. As I climbed the stairs I could sense the excitement hanging in the air like bats. Sonar bounced off me like sleet, echo-locating the birthday boy. I opened the door like everything was normal.

"Surprise!" screamed the sofa.

"Surprise!" screamed the refrigerator.

"Surprise!" screamed the brown stain on the rug.

"Surprise!" screamed the bathroom fixtures in unison.

"Surprise!" screamed the little plastic flowers in the peacock-blue vase with one cartoon mouse voice.

"You guys," I said.

Kona Lowell

About the Author

Kona Lowell hides out on the Big Island, Hawaii, way up in the mist, with his wife, Chee, their Jellicle cat Kiko and their somewhat cat-like creature, Popo. He is also the author of the popular parody website *The Dolphin Sky Foundation* and the creator of its central epic character, Akiryon Baba Yat, the Moe Howard of ascended masters. When he is not writing, Kona is asleep. Please be quiet.

Printed in the United States
742800004B